"It could be I was wrong about you. I thought you were sweet,"

Shelby told Jake, wounded.

"I am. On you," he admitted.

"Oh, Jake!" she murmured, defensiveness melting as she saw it from his point of view. "I'm sorry."

"Don't be. You're the one with the hole in your heart." Hunkered down beside her chair, Jake tucked a curl behind her ear, traced the tear track and then her bottom lip with the flat of his thumb.

Shelby trapped his hand with both of hers. But it was a poor defense mechanism, for he let her keep it, leaned in and stole a kiss. It sparked heat lightning across the stormy expanse of her heart. Fiercely, she blinked tear-shine, crowded out rational thought and kissed him back.

Books by Susan Kirby

Love Inspired

Your Dream and Mine #64
Love Sign #127

SUSAN KIRBY

has written numerous novels for children, teens and adults. She is a recipient of the Child Study Children's Book Committee Award, and has received honors from The Friends of American Writers. Her Main Street Series for children, a collection of books that follow one family through four generations of living along the famed highway Route 66, has enjoyed popularity with children and adults alike. With a number of historical novels to her credit, Susan enjoys intermingling writing and research travels with visits to classrooms across the country.

Love Sign
Susan Kirby

Published by Steeple Hill Books™

STEEPLE HILL BOOKS

ISBN 0-373-87134-1

LOVE SIGN

Visit us at www.steeplehill.com

Printed in U.S.A.

For in Him we live and move and have our being.
—*Acts* 17:28

To Levi
You're a patient sounding board
a storehouse of ideas
and a constant source of joy.
What more could a mother ask?

Chapter One

Shelby Taylor awoke ahead of her alarm. She slipped out of bed and onto her knees. Words were slow to come, but time spent with God quieted her hurting heart. She rose to turn off her alarm and open the drapes. The bedroom window of her third-story Lake Shore Drive apartment overlooked Lake Michigan. A kiss-me red sunrise splashed rosy hues over whitecaps, gulls and bobbing sailboats. Shelby dawdled, combing her fingers through short red-gold tangles and admiring God's artistry as if it were an ordinary Saturday and as if time were a luxury she could afford. But her calendar told a different story. She flipped the page to July, covering the unnecessary reminder of what was *not* going to happen this last weekend in June.

Shelby plugged in the coffeemaker, showered, then swung her closet door wide. White satin and lace spilled out and tickled her in the ribs. She stood clutching a damp towel, waiting for the aftershocks to subside. She should do something with the dress.

But what? Shelby retreated to the kitchen, braced herself with coffee and returned to the closet. She skimmed past the wedding gown and retrieved a streamlined skirt and silk blouse.

Patrick Delaney, a corporate attorney, had been a part of her life for three years. Shelby had come to appreciate him as a realist who knew his limitations. *Until he called off their wedding with only a week left on the clock.*

Shelby didn't plead or storm or try to bury him in guilt. An only child with busy parents who were intent on not spoiling her, she had been conditioned at any early age to hold back the little actress within. "Scenes" belonged in childhood plays and daydreams and storybooks.

It was a lesson that served her well as an editor, as a writer and even as a jilted bride. While juggling wedding cancellations and a nightmarish problem with an author who was threatening a lawsuit because she didn't like her book cover, Shelby had hugged the small consolation that someday, this week of horror would provide grist for the mill. That, God's grace and the promise of the only thing she hadn't canceled—weekend reservations at Wildwood—had kept her going.

Chosen initially as a honeymoon getaway, Wildwood was a downstate bed-and-breakfast with cozy cottages off in the pines. She prayed it would prove the perfect hideaway to the plot her new novel, which hereto was not stewing so well.

Shelby lifted her eyes to the shelf on the wall facing her computer. Her Bible was there, and five teen novels with her own name on the binding. If not for the meat-and-potato necessities of the real world, she would be writing full-time.

Shelby packed light and pulled her game face from her cosmetic bag, beginning with sunblock. Hazel eyed and fair skinned, she burned easily if she spent much time outdoors. While that hadn't been a problem in some time, her new laptop computer gave her options, sunshine among them. Feeling more composed, more focused and better equipped to cope, she donned a pair of trendy platform sandals and pearl earrings. Shelby finished her coffee standing up before stuffing projects from work into an oversize book bag. *Anesthesia, should her own fiction fail her.*

A fresh breeze whisked through Jackson Signs South. It diluted the blended odor of dust, engine grease, sweeping compound and banner ink. Jake Jackson hit the remote. The overhead chain-driven door shuddered up the track. Jake shifted the fifty-foot ladder truck into gear, then braked for his twelve-year-old niece, Joy, who blocked his way with her skinny arms outstretched.

He cranked down the window. "You trying to get run over, blondie?"

Straw-haired and freckled, Joy wrinkled her nose at the outgrown nickname. "Just checking your brakes. Is Mom around?"

Jake jerked his thumb toward the back room where his oldest sister, Paula, was bending neon. "Thought you'd be in the field."

"Mr. Wiseman never showed up. We waited an hour."

"Something must have kept him." Jake anchored

the stack of service orders on the seat beside him with a phone book. "Move it or lose it, kiddo. I have a bank job waiting."

"How about a ride home?" Joy asked.

"Okay," Jake agreed. "Update your mom first, and let's go."

Joy flung her hoe on the back of the flatbed crane truck, trotted into the neon room and was back in short order. "Can we swing by the sign first?"

"What sign?" Jake played dumb.

"*Dad's* sign."

Jake was concerned over Joy's johnny-come-lately fascination with her absentee father, Colton Blake. Fifteen years ago Colton's image had gone up on the billboard on the outskirts of Liberty Flats after Wind, Water and Sky Outdoor Gear chose him for their advertising campaign. Clad in jeans, flannel, leather boots and a distinguishing red voyager cap, the Voyager, as Colton was dubbed, had become a North American icon in the intervening years—all due to that one billboard image of him paddling a canoe along a wilderness stream.

"Satisfied?" Jake asked as they cruised past.

"Thanks," Joy said, attention riveted on the bigger-than-life portrait of the father she had never met. "Uncle Jake?" she began. "Dad has a right to know about me, don't you think?"

"It's not my call," replied Jake.

Joy flopped against the seat. "You're a big help."

Jake took her mood shift in stride. She had been underfoot since she could crawl. But then with Colton gone and her mother sharing the sign company partnership, where else would she be?

* * *

The interstate highway gave way to a fair-size city 150 miles south of Chicago. Shelby spotted a bank from the off-ramp. A lighted message board spelled out generous savings rates—the decimal point was missing.

A sign truck turned into the lot just ahead of her. It rolled to a stop and parallel parked at the curb in front of the bank. The driver cut the motor and climbed out, a lanky, wide-shouldered, long-waisted man in jeans and T-shirt, dark glasses and a baseball cap.

Shelby circled the lot once before finding a space. She searched her shoulder bag for her traveler's checks, only to remember they were in her suitcase.

The sun was hot and climbing as Shelby opened the trunk. She grabbed her suitcase, returned to the front seat to retrieve her traveler's checks from within, then locked the car, leaving the suitcase on the seat with her laptop.

The sign serviceman was up on the back of the flatbed truck raising his hydraulic ladder as Shelby approached the curb on the heels of a heavyset fellow in painter's garb. "Better buy CDs. The rates are about to take a dive," the sign man called to the painter.

"Go home, Jake, you old spoiler, you," replied the grinning painter, then held the door for Shelby.

Waiting in line, Shelby's attention strayed inward to that place where stories were born. First, a name. Something catchy for the heroine. She entertained a dozen possibilities in the time it took to cash a traveler's check and let herself out again. The ladder on the sign truck stretched to the roof of the building.

Shelby cut around the truck, off the curb and onto asphalt.

"Look out, lady! Stay back!"

Shelby pivoted to see the sign truck's hydraulic ladder swing away from the building, leaving the sign man on the roof, waving, shouting a warning. Alarmed, Shelby leapt back onto the curb and watched the unmanned ladder sweep the air twenty feet above the parking lot. All at once, the boom toppled. It came down like a limb in an ice storm and unbalanced the truck. The truck tilted, then fell over on its side. The boom crashed into Shelby's car with a stomach-turning crunch of steel and shattering glass.

When the dust settled, what lay beneath the crane more closely resembled a crumpled soda can than a car. The air fizzed out of a tire, rupturing the caught-breath silence. Shelby wheeled around, tipping her face to the sign man hunkered at the edge of the roof.

"It's never done that before," he said, peering down at the damage. "Some kind of malfunction..."

"*You* or the crane?" Shelby cut in.

"Toggle switch, I'm guessing." He shifted to his feet and planted his hands on narrow hips. His sunglasses and the brim of his cap shadowed a tanned and wary demeanor. "I'm sorry. I don't know what else to say."

It was a car, not a human being. *Or a relationship squashed like a bug.* As Shelby struggled with herself, the young man palmed his cap and dived tanned fingers through short-clipped sun-bleached chestnut waves. "I hate to ask. But could you help me down?" he ventured. "There's a rope there—fell off the deck."

"Deck?"

"Truck deck," he amended, pointing.

Shelby cast the less-than-stable-looking truck a doubtful glance. "It won't roll over on me, will it?"

"It shouldn't."

Peachy. The rope had fallen on the pavement when the truck spilled over. Shelby gripped her purse under one arm and picked up one end of the rope.

"Can you throw me one end?" Sign Man called from the roof.

Shelby gave it a go. The rope uncurled like a striking snake. It climbed half a story, then dropped and nipped her on the noggin. Her second effort was better, but unsuccessful. She put her shoulder bag down on the curb.

A pickup truck pulled into the parking lot. The man inside assessed the situation and climbed out. "Anyone hurt?" he asked.

"Just my car," said Shelby ruefully.

"Here, let me," he said, and took the rope.

Relieved, Shelby backed out of the way and dusted her hands.

The man coiled the rope a few times and tossed it skyward. Sign Man caught it and anchored his end. The muscles in his arms bunched as he eased himself down the rope and to the ground.

He was thirtyish, clean-shaven with strong shoulders and tall enough so that Shelby had to look up. The sunglasses still screened his eyes. He pressed his lips together, and dimples emerged then went into hiding again as he shifted his attention to the man who had come to their aid. With tanned and capable hands, he slipped the sunglasses from his face and into his T-shirt pocket as he thanked the Good Samaritan.

"The hydraulic lever stuck. I figured the crane

would circle around and come back to me," he explained. "I didn't think about it jerking the truck over."

"Did you set your outriggers?" asked the other man.

"Just on the driver's side. I know better. I got distracted and broke my own rules." Sign Man's glance shifted to Shelby. His eyes, a striking blue, enhanced prominent cheeks. His jaw sloped to a nicely carved chin that jutted slightly as he asked, "Are you in a hurry to get someplace?"

"No. Not now," replied Shelby.

"I'll call one of my men and get this truck upright," he said. "Then I'll see what we can do about getting you wherever you're headed."

"Wildwood," she said.

"Vacationing?" he asked.

Shelby nodded, and glanced at the Good Samaritan who was walking away. Sign Man noticed, and called after him, "Thanks, man."

The man waved and drove away in his pickup truck.

It wasn't long until a second sign truck pulled into the lot in answer to Sign Man's phone call. With the help of the crane, the truck was soon upright and the boom off Shelby's car.

Sign Man retrieved Shelby's purse from the curb on his way by. "Here you go," he said. Faint creases tugged at the corners of his morning glory eyes. "I'm Jake Jackson."

"Shelby Taylor," she returned.

Jake started to offer his hand, then checked the impulse. He turned up a grease-smudged palm and asked, "So how upset are you?"

"I'm sorry I snapped at you." Lamely, Shelby offered, "It happened so fast."

"Kind of caught me off guard, too." He spared her further apology and glanced back at her car. "I'll call my insurance company, see if they can get you something to drive," he offered.

Jake called on his cell phone and returned with word that his insurer would send an adjuster out. "He'll see about a loaner car once he has taken some pictures and squared away the paperwork. Like I said, I'd be happy to give you a lift if you don't want to wait on him."

At a loss as to how else she was to reach the cabin at Wildwood, Shelby accepted.

"Need anything from the car?" he asked.

"My laptop and suitcase from the front seat. Grab my cell phone, too, would you? Oh! And my book bag, please. It's in the trunk," she said, and gave him her car keys.

Jake jerked a thumb in the direction of the bank lobby. "May as well wait inside where it's cool," he said.

Thoughtful, as saboteurs went, noted Shelby as she retreated to the lobby. He wasn't long. Her suitcase swung from one hand, her laptop from the other. He retrieved her cell phone from his shirt pocket. Their fingers brushed as it changed hands.

"Can you get along without the book bag? I didn't have any luck popping the trunk lid," he said.

Reluctant to leave unpublished works behind, Shelby wondered aloud, "Could we pry it open?"

"I thought of that. But the adjuster may want to snap his pictures before we tear into it," he said.

Conceding his point, Shelby followed him to his

truck. He checked the oil, then wiped his hands on a towel that lay in the seat. Except for some scraped paint and a broken side view mirror, the truck appeared sound. The engine coughed a time or two en route to the sign shop. But they covered the short distance without incident.

Shelby's gaze swept twin steel buildings, a hodge-podge of equipment emblazoned with the Jackson name, and a graveyard of old signs.

"It's a family business," Jake explained. "We have a shop south of here at Liberty Flats. Wildwood's just a few miles farther on. Hope I haven't fouled up your vacation too badly."

"It's a working one, anyway." Shelby accepted his help out of the truck. He had a steady hand. Durable fingers, a callused palm and a measured grip. She turned to collect her things.

"Let me." Jake reached for her suitcase and laptop.

Shelby followed him to a sporty four-wheel drive vehicle and stowed her things behind the seat while she climbed in.

"There's a bookstore nearby. You want to pick up something to read?" he asked as they got underway.

Realizing he had misunderstood about the book bag, she said, "Thanks, but it isn't leisure reading. The bag contains manuscripts."

"You're a writer?" Jake winced as she conceded as much. "Can't say I'd want to leave *my* life's work in the trunk of a wrecked car."

"It isn't mine." Seeing his confusion, Shelby explained, "I work full-time for Parnell Publishing, and write part-time. What will they do with the car?"

"Have it towed, I suppose. I'll phone the insurance company again and explain about the manuscripts. They could take it to my shop. It'd be easier for you to access than at a salvage yard.''

Jake made the call while waiting for a light to change. Traffic flowed once more. He resumed their conversation. ''What is it you do at Parnell?''

''I'm an editor.''

''Really! Can't say I've ever met an editor.'' Jake threaded his way along busy streets. ''What kind of books does your company publish?''

''We do a variety of nonfiction titles—self-help, how-tos, food and cooking titles, home and family, travel and guidebooks. That sort of thing,'' said Shelby.

''And your part-time writing—is that for Parnell?''

''No. I write romance mysteries for young adults.''

''Is that right?'' His smile deepened, his eyes reflecting a sunny twinkle. ''Thomasina's a real fan of romance novels. Out at Wildwood,'' he added. ''She and her husband Trace have transformed that old farm into a real cozy vacation retreat.''

''I've heard nothing but good things about their business,'' said Shelby as Jake took the interstate south out of town. ''I look forward to meeting them.''

''You'll have to stick around a couple of weeks, then. They left for the southwest two days ago for their third wedding anniversary.

''Oh.''

''How about you? Are you married?'' he asked with a glance from those vivid blue eyes.

''No.''

''Seeing someone?''

"No." The word to Shelby's own ears, clanged like a metal gate. She twisted the strap of her pocket book, and fell silent.

They passed the next dozen miles in silence. Jake flipped the air off as they exited the interstate, trucked past the Voyager billboard, and rolled down the window as they skirted Liberty Flats.

"Too much wind? I can roll it up," offered Jake, as the breeze riffled Shelby's short curls.

"No, don't. It's fine," she said and lowered her window, too.

Jake stole a sidelong glance, admiring the wind in her hair and sunlight dancing on flawless skin. But he couldn't remember when he had seen such a soft round face look so long and weary. His carelessness had complicated her vacation plans, big time, that went without saying. He thought about apologizing again. But then, what good did that do? They hurtled along the country road a few miles, then Jake slowed for Wildwood Lane.

Shelby draped her arm out the window, letting the air blow through her fingers. In the air there was a fragrance of green growing things and of sun-warmed earth. She breathed deeply, filling her lungs with clean country air, willing the stone to roll off her heart. Time, that's what she needed. Anonymity in which to lick her wounds until she had ceased to flinch at words like *marriage* and *anniversary*.

The lane ended in front of a two-story farmhouse. The house, freshly painted, gleamed like a pearl amidst blooming gardens and barn-red outbuildings. Reprieve was so close, she could almost taste it.

"Go on and get squared away. I'll bring your things," Jake offered.

The path to the front office was bordered by a bright tangle of nodding flowers. Inside, flowerpots filled the office windowsills. Trailing plants spilled from the pots onto a battered drop-leaf table. There was a coffee urn and cups and glasses and iced lemonade beading a carnival glass pitcher. Shelby pushed the bell. Chimes rang through the house. She helped herself to a glass of lemonade. A young woman came in response to the bell. "May I help you?" she asked, her hoop earrings jangling.

"Yes, I have reservations." Shelby gave her her name.

The woman sat down at the computer and hit a few keys. When she lifted her yes again, her smile had faded. "I'm sorry. But I don't seem to have any record of it," she said.

Shelby set down the half-drained glass of lemonade to retrieve the confirmation number from her checkbook register where she had written it on the day she and Patrick finalized their honeymoon plans.

The young woman typed in the number. Frown lines creased her forehead. "You're marked out."

Startled, Shelby protested, "There must be some mistake."

"Forgive me, you're right, it wasn't you." The young woman turned from the screen to a lined tablet. "It was a man who called to cancel. I wrote it here somewhere." She ran a finger down to the middle of the page and looked up again. "Patrick Delaney."

The name washed over Shelby in a bone-skinning tide. Tears threatened. She batted them back, struggling to make mental adjustments. "If the cottage has been rented, a room will do."

"I'm sorry, but we're booked here at the house, too."

Jake was a dozen steps from the house when the front door spit Shelby out onto the garden path. Her cream-colored silk blouse and a fitted skirt molded nicely to feminine curves.

She was almost upon him before she saw him and skidded to a stop. Clouds darkened her eyes. She pressed her full lips together. A pulse hammered at her smooth, white temples.

"There's been a mix-up. I hate to ask, but could I please have a ride back to town?" she said, and reached for her laptop.

Her effort to keep it together as the morning went from bad to worse put a commiserating knot in Jake's gut. But her guarded facade warned him against a barrage of questions. He passed her the laptop. Fumbling to take the suitcase, too, she shifted her pocketbook and reached for the suitcase handle.

"Go on, I'll bring it," said Jake quickly.

She nodded and turned toward the drive. Jake watched the hem of her skirt trail over tall flowers that sweetened the path. She crossed crushed rock, climbed into the Jeep and settled there, hugging her laptop. Jake rubbed an uncomfortable sensation in his chest, then set her suitcase down and went inside.

"'Morning, Annie."

Antoinette Penn smiled a welcome from behind the desk. "Hello, Jake. If you're looking for Trace, he's not here."

"I'd heard they'd taken off," he said and took off his cap. "What happened with Shelby Taylor's reservations?"

"A guy called this morning and canceled the reservations," explained Antoinette.

"But if *she* made the reservations..." began Jake.

"For all I know, they made them together," Antoinette interjected. "Honeymoons are usually planned that way."

Startled, Jake blurted, "Honeymoon? She's getting married?"

"Not anymore. He called it off. That's the reason he gave for canceling."

Shelby's fragile state fell in place like a key fitting tumblers. "So what's she doing here?" he asked.

"I don't know, Jake. All I know is the honeymoon cottage is taken."

Jake swung around and looked out the window. Shelby's slim arms were still wrapped around her laptop. He had done all he could. And yet....Jake shifted his feet. "How about a room here in the house?"

"Sorry. It's like I told her, we're booked."

"What about Trace and Thomasina's room? They won't be needing it," he reasoned.

"It's full of their stuff!"

"Under the circumstances, she may not mind."

"I wasn't talking about *her*." Antoinette drew herself up. "What're you trying to do—get me fired?"

"Oh, come on," Jake cajoled. "What's the point in being in charge if you can't make an executive decision?"

"Save your breath, Jake. I am *not* booking Trace and Thomasina's bedroom. And you can quit looking at me like that, it's not my fault," huffed Antoinette.

"She's shell-shocked," Jake said. "Jilted, canceled and I dropped the crane on her car."

"You what?"

"Never mind. Guess I better drive her back to town."

"I wish you would," said Antoinette, rubbing her temples. "She's making my head throb."

"Mine, too," Jake said. Though on closer accounting, it was more of a burn than a throb and it wasn't confined to his head. He rubbed his chest again, reached into his pocket for an antacid tablet and left Antoinette muttering.

Chapter Two

Jake was gone so long, Shelby grew restless. She climbed out of the Jeep and was almost to the farmhouse screen door when she overheard his parting exchange with the desk clerk. He swung out onto the path before she could patch her expression.

Jake blinked finding her there and tipped his cap back, a gesture Shelby was beginning to recognize as habitual.

"No vacancies," she filled the sudden caught-breath silence.

"Antoinette told me. I said I'd get that," he said and reached for her suitcase on the walk where he had left it.

"I had a thought while I was waiting...perhaps a room in Liberty Flats," said Shelby, following him toward the Jeep.

"There's no motel. It's a pretty small town," he said.

Shelby raked her fingers through her curls. Anxious to find herself a place before he began to regard her as a pup he had orphaned and could not leave to fend for herself, she asked, "What about Bloomington?"

"Sure. There are plenty of rooms there if that's what you want to do," he said, and opened the Jeep door for her.

Shelby plucked her laptop off the seat and slid in. Jake circled to the driver's side and put her suitcase behind the seat. He would have stowed her laptop there, too, except she had her arms around it again. "Wherever you want to go. Just name it," he said, as he climbed behind the wheel.

"Somewhere quiet where I can work. Speaking of which, I'm keeping you from yours," she said.

"I was due for a morning off."

"Not like this," said Shelby.

"We've had a nice ride so far," said Jake.

"Thanks," she said with a wan smile.

"For what?"

"Being such a gentleman."

Her attitude caught Jake off guard. Feeling all the more responsible for her predicament, he said, "There's plenty of room at my grandmother's house. You'd be welcome to stay."

"Oh, no. I couldn't impose," she said hastily.

"You wouldn't be. Gram Kate likes having company."

"That's kind. But it's too much to ask."

"You didn't ask. I offered." Hoping she would accept and relieve his conscience, Jake stopped at the crossroads just shy of Liberty Flats. His turn was dependent upon her decision. "Would you like to have a look before you make up your mind?"

Shelby's head was pounding. She anchored the

laptop between her feet on the floor and reached into her shoulder bag. "Here," she said, and uncapped a bottle of aspirin.

"What's this?"

"For your headache. Mine's splitting, too."

Chagrined Jake rubbed the back of his neck. "You have good ears," he said finally.

"So I've heard." Shelby shook two tablets into her palm and offered them, saying, "My treat."

She was a treat, dressed all in cream. All that kept Jake from telling her so was the pain in her doe-soft hazel eyes and a mouth that was too grave. That quick, she got to him. *An almost-could-have-been-should-have-been-married woman.* He thanked God she wasn't, and gestured, saying, "You first."

Shelby tossed the tablets back. They burned all the way down. She coughed and rubbed her eyes. Jake pushed a box of tissues her way. Hoping for the chance to know her better, he made the turn into Liberty Flats. "I'll get you something to wash it down with."

The shady streets spanned a time line of American housing, from Victorian to cheerful bungalows to ranch-style homes to imposing Cape Cods on manicured lawns. At the center of town, Jake circled the village green. It enfolded a bandstand, picnic tables, a memorial stone honoring war dead and a flag pole. Old Glory rippled in the breeze, a twin to the flag jutting from the brick front of Newt's Market across the way. The remainder of the business district consisted of boarded-up buildings, a few of which leaned like stacked stove wood.

Jake turned the Jeep up the alley and parked in the driveway of his timber-framed shop. Shelby spotted the sign company logo above the overhead door. The Jackson name was also lettered on the side of the building. "You live here, too?" she asked.

"I have lately. Gram's memory isn't what it used to be," said Jake. "My sisters have families to look after. All but the youngest, and she just got married. I was the logical choice. Come on, and I'll get you that drink."

His amiable smile tweezed the thorn that had cropped up at Shelby's realization the house he referred to as his grandmother's was his home, too. She climbed out and paused for a closer look at the house. It was a two-story arts-and-craft home with clean lines and deep verandas. The slate roof sloped away from a catwalk enclosed by a wrought iron railing.

Jake knocked the dust off his feet on the back veranda and waited for her to catch up. The back door opened into a eclectic kitchen that spanned a generation. *Good bones, nice texture.* In her head Shelby heard her mother accentuating the positive.

"Tea? Juice? Soda?" Jake offered, his footsteps ringing over vintage pine flooring.

"Water's fine." Shelby dropped her head back, admiring a high ceiling sectioned by hand-hewn oak beams. The room was long and wide and graced with deep windows. Fresh flowers adorned a table big enough for all the king's horses and men. Handicrafts decorated the walls—a framed wood-burned copy of the Lord's Prayer, a plaque inscribed Friends Are Special People. The napkin holder had rust spots, and child-size fingerprints glazed the cookie jar.

Jake drew her a glass of water, waited as she drained it and returned the empty glass to the sink.

"It's a restful house. Don't think I'm not tempted to accept your hospitality," Shelby began. Then Jake's beeper cut in. She gestured, saying, "Go ahead. Don't let me keep you."

Jake excused himself to make a phone call.

After the chaos of the morning, the quiet house was to Shelby what oil was to chafed skin. Her eye skipped from child-crafted refrigerator art to toast crumbs on the counter to the yellow energy efficiency rating sticker, the grease-splattered corners of which curled from the surface of a new stove. *Ordinary folk, cutting corners rushing through ordinary days.* It wasn't like her to impose on the kindness of strangers. But then again, she hadn't exactly been herself lately.

"Shall I bring in your things, or do you want a ride back to town?" asked Jake, returning.

"Are you sure I won't be in the way?" Shelby asked.

"I'm sure," he said.

"I can see you're a busy man. I won't be a pest," she promised.

Jake smiled and excused himself and returned moments later with her belongings. "This way."

Shelby let go the last vestiges of convention and trekked after him through the kitchen and dining room. Their footsteps fell to a whisper on the rose carpet that spanned the staircase. The woodwork was dark, the walls embossed, the decor turn-of-the-century elegant, though with a nice splash of modern graces.

The guest room at the top of the landing was spacious and homey with quilts and lace curtains and woven rugs. Shelby circled the room, absorbing it with an appreciative glance that didn't escape Jake. "My mother would love this. She works with Harbor House, restoring old houses for low-income families," she said.

"And your father?"

"He is a plastic surgeon."

"I'll bet even he couldn't put a pretty face on this day," said Jake in open sympathy.

"I should have seen it coming," she murmured, then flushed at his confusion. "Oh! You mean the car."

He nodded. "What'd you think?"

Patrick. She thought he meant Patrick. Embarrassed, Shelby averted her face.

"Can I get you anything?" asked Jake.

"I'm fine, thanks," she said, gripping her pocketbook.

"Okay. I need to be going. But if you need anything, my sister Paula is out back in the shop," Jake told her.

"I'll be fine," she said. "Thank you, Mr. Jackson."

"Glad to help," he said, and stopped in the door to look back. "And make that Jake."

"Jake," Shelby amended, meeting his gaze. His smiling eyes begged descriptive notation: *Pale tropical waters splashing at sun-browned banks.*

No wastrel of words, Shelby filed the line away for literary use. She rubbed her throbbing temples, slipped out of her platform sandals and stretched out on the bed. It was plush and cozy and comforting. But she couldn't relax. She hadn't in days. Locking her hands behind her head, she invited a story line to wander in and make order of her muddled thoughts. But before she could conjure up any story characters a slim, attractive, auburn-haired woman in a cotton shirt and jeans knocked at the open door.

"You must be Shelby. Don't get up. Just popped in to say hi." A smiled warmed her face. "There's ham and fruit in the refrigerator. Help yourself when you get hungry."

"That's kind of you, thank you, but I'll get something out."

"There is no 'out.' Except Newt's Market, and you'll soon tire of that. I'm Paula Blake, by the way. Jake's sister."

"He mentioned you," Shelby said. She introduced herself.

"Jake says you write and edit and all sorts of interesting things," Paula continued amiably. "Excuse me while I get that."

Shelby swung her feet off the bed and into her shoes as Paula crossed to the nightstand and the ringing phone.

"I'm sure there's a perfectly logical explanation, Joy," Paula said. "Give Mr. Wiseman a break, would you? No, Dirk can't come over. I'll see you at four. I love you. Bye-bye.

"My daughter," Paula explained, hanging up the phone. "She's doing some field work over her summer vacation. Or supposed to be. Her boss didn't pick her up this morning. His van is gone. She can't reach him on the phone, now she's conjuring wild scenarios. He's sick. He's lost. He's fallen and can't get up," Paula ticked Joy fancies off on her fingers and rolled eyes as blue as Jake's. "Kids! Now be sure and eat something," she continued without stopping for breath, and backed out of the door, still talking.

The silence in Paula's wake was nagging. Shelby found her way to the bathroom, tidied up and went downstairs. She made a sandwich, washed it down with a soda, then returned to her room and set up her laptop. Once upon a time...she told herself, fingers poised and waiting. The anticipated lights did not flash. No icons. No whirring. Just a black screen.

"Come on, come on," murmured Shelby. "Give me a break. Please?" she muttered. But the screen remained dark and cold. At length, Shelby gave up. She fished pad and pen and dime-store reading glasses from her shoulder bag, took a seat and tried to recall the idea she had had before Patrick pushed the lead domino and brought her well-ordered future tumbling down around her. But her thought screen was as blank as her computer screen.

Shelby grumbled and wandered to the window and hiked it. She tapped folded glasses against the frame. Voilà! As if by design, a girl rode into the alley below, then flung her bicycle down. A skinny, sunburned, straw-haired preteen in cutoff jeans, she pinched off hollyhocks greens with bright-tipped fingernails and left a shredded trail of leaves into Jake's shop. Moments later, she reappeared with Paula at her heels. Paula turned the girl toward a vegetable patch and gave her a nudge.

"But Mom! I don't even like vegetables." The girl's voice carried through the open window. "Yikes! A bee! I think I'm allergic! Well, I *could* be. M-o-o-o-m!" she wailed, hands on skinny hips. "Oh, all right! How much are you paying me?"

"A nickel a weed," Paula said.

"A nickel? Is that all?"

"Make it a penny," Paula returned.

"Mom!"

"Keep whining, Joy, and you'll be weeding for free." Paula retreated into the shop.

Shelby pressed her nose to the window screen and watched Joy flounce over the garden. She plucked a weed here, a weed there, all hop-and-stop energy with no logical system. It was hard to picture a girl like that willingly weeding fields that ran on for acres and acres.

So what made Joy tick? What movements turned behind those eyes and turned-up nose and sullen brow? Shelby played what-if until a distant rumbling broke her concentration. Cool air rose from a vent on the floor below the window. Air-conditioning.

Shelby closed the window, took the chair again and balanced the pad on her knee. An opening sentence trickled across the page to be joined by more words, inserted here and there until it became a nice fat paragraph. She reached for her glasses.

Cranes, crushed cars, trapped book bags and blue-eyed men retreated as a Joy-like girl in frayed shorts and peeling freckles appeared on the lined yellow tablet. A Patrick-like guy took shape beside her. The resemblance startled Shelby from fiction to reality. She hadn't deliberately chosen him for inspiration. It was automatic. Finger memory, like a pianist's hands finding the right keys when the pages to a familiar song fluttered shut.

Shelby marked out the Patrick clone and reeled through male acquaintances, seeking hero inspiration elsewhere. None seemed to fit. Again, the Patrick-like character beckoned. Stubbornly resisting, she stirred from her chair and paced to the window. Sunshine glittered off the nearby building, lighting the lettering on the side of the building: Jackson Signs South.

Jake Jackson. He had been kind. Helpful. Patient. A gentleman. The heroics of everyday life. And he had those arresting eyes. Here, here! Her heart might be curled into the fetal position, but she still had her story world. A world with a voracious appetite, it fed indiscriminately on new situations, new people, fresh material to keep her upright and writing. That was the upside of this unsettling, upside down day. "This is the day the Lord has made."

The snippet of verse ran through Shelby's head. Not the day she had expected or long anticipated, rather a day marked by adversity. Yet in God's hands, even shrapnel was a windfall, a deposit, a hedge against creative bankruptcy.

Shelby added Jake to her characters cast. She reshaped him into a seventeen-year-old in studious dark-rimmed glasses with a knack for mystery solving and a love for dirt-track racing.

A leggy raven-haired beauty barged onto the page. Tara. Before Shelby's delighted eyes, Tara challenged her Joy-like character for the hero's heart. Sparks flew better in triangles. No sparks. No conflict. No story. Not a problem today. The words flowed, the headache fled.

Thank you, Lord. Thank you. You always know just what I need.

Chapter Three

It had been a while since Jake had met a woman who interested him enough to make the day stretch long. He played catch-up all afternoon and fell several jobs short of completing his service calls. By the time he returned to the Bloomington shop, his crew had left for the day.

Two brothers-in-law worked with him in the erecting and servicing of signs. A third oversaw the computerized banners in the Liberty Flats shop while Paula shaped neon for custom-made signs. It was a skill both she and Jake had learned from their father, John Jackson.

A two-car automobile accident had claimed Jake's parents' lives when Jake was nineteen. Colton, Paula's husband of just a few weeks, had been at the wheel of the second car, and had escaped with minor injuries. With his parents gone, and Paula's marriage on the rocks as quickly as it had come together, it was only by the grace of God that Gram Kate had kept the family together, and the sign company, too.

Now, a dozen years later, Jackson Signs was thriving.

Recently Paula had transferred all their records onto computer. She had taken some classes and was at ease with the new system. Jake wasn't. But he did appreciate the options gained by linking the sign shops and their home offices. Now, he could go home and relax a while before entering the day's business.

Jake locked up the shop, stopped for chicken and the fixings, then took the highway south. Once home, he put supper in the oven on low, set the table and climbed the stairs. The second-story landing circled past the guest room. Shelby's door was closed. Jake grabbed clean clothes and closed himself into the upstairs bathroom to shower and change.

The whistled rendition of a catchy advertising jingle penetrated Shelby's subconscious. By and by, the hum of an electric razor muted the cheery tune. Shelby sank back into to her story only to emerge again when the whistling ceased. The razor was quiet, too. Focus broken, she rose on cramped limbs and crossed to the door.

Jake was at the top of the stairs. A short-sleeved navy-blue shirt hugged the contours of muscles that flexed as he tucked his shirttail into his jeans. The denim, faded and softened by wash and wear, suited the lean, fit lines of his body as he turned and surprised her watching him from the open door.

"I heard you whistling."

"Was I?" He smiled. "Hope I didn't disturb you."

"Not at all," Shelby said.

His dimples deepened. There was a sheen to his clean-shaven jaw that caught the light. His hair was damp from the shower and bore the tracks of a comb. "Are you ready for dinner?" he asked.

"If you'll let me help," she offered.

"No need, it's on the table."

"Next time, call me and I'll help," said Shelby, flushing. "I guess I should have warned you—when I'm writing, everything fades away. Time. Good intentions, everything."

"It'll stand you in good stead in this house," Jake replied. "Family tracking in and out at all hours. It can turn into a regular zoo if you don't hold your mouth just right."

Shelby noted his was nicely held. His eyes, too. The dark shirt heightened their striking hue. The observation was part of her craft, a writing thing, as natural as breathing. She smelled soap, and something else, too. Something tantalizing. *Or was that dinner?* Since the breakup, Shelby had almost forgotten what hunger felt like. Her stomach gave a sharp reminder. "I'll be right down." Quickly, she retreated to tidy up after herself.

Jake waited for her, watching from the open door as she gathered the paper wads strewn about her chair. In contrast to those carelessly scattered papers was the precision with which she aligned her notebook, pen and reading glasses on the dresser.

"You write in long hand?" Jake asked as she snapped off the reading lamp.

"Not as a rule. But my laptop is on the fritz."

"Not another crane casualty," he said and clucked his tongue.

"There's not a scratch on it," replied Shelby. "It

may just be a glitch. I'm not much good at trouble-shooting.''

"I'll take a look if you like," he offered.

"Would you mind? I'd really appreciate it," Shelby said.

"After dinner, then. I hope you like chicken," he added.

"I do," she returned, closing the door behind her. "But you shouldn't have gone to so much trouble."

"I didn't. It's carryout. Except for the tomatoes."

"I noticed the garden from the window," Shelby told him.

"Green-thumb therapy," Jake said. He held up his thumb and motioned for her to precede him down the stairs. "What about you? Do you garden?"

"I live in a third-floor apartment. But I planted blue lobelia and vincas in a window box this year."

"Flowers, right?" he asked, and followed her down, momentarily distracted by the muted flame of red-gold curls against her slim white neck. He caught himself wondering if her skin was as soft to touch as it was to the eyes, and admitted, "Mostly what I know about flowers is that mowing them down gets you in trouble."

Flowers. They had been Patrick's passion. Shelby caught herself one foot down memory lane. She took her mind by the edges, gave it a shake and followed Jake into the kitchen where he introduced her to his grandmother, Kate Grisham.

Kate had hair like spun wool and a round face, powdered and wrinkled. Her lips were painted outside the lines. They tilted as she greeted Shelby, saying, "How lovely to meet you."

"Shelby works with books," Jake told her.

"You're Jake's bookkeeper!" Gram Kate set a pitcher of tea on the table and came to Shelby with hands outstretched.

"She doesn't work for me, Gram. We met at the bank." Jake went on to explain about the accident.

"Thank goodness you weren't hurt," Gram said, slow to release Shelby's hands. "Jake, dear you must be more careful! Why, I hate to think what might have happened if that... Joy needs... Next time you mustn't..."

The flow of Gram's words stopped. She peered more closely at Shelby, dismissed her lost train of thought and patted her hair.

"Ready to eat, Gram?" Jake asked gently, and seated her. Declining Shelby's help in transferring food from the oven to the table, he seated her, too, and when the food was in place, took his own chair.

Shelby spread her napkin over her lap. Gram Kate reached for her hand. "Would you ask the blessing for us, dear?" she asked, and patted Shelby's fingers.

Shelby tucked her chin. "Heavenly Father..."

"Dear God," rumbled Jake.

They both stopped and looked up.

"Don't tease your sister. Take her hand, now Jake, and say grace before the ice me—me-malts," said Gram Kate, her tone sweetly chiding.

It was no hardship for Jake. He took Shelby's hand, and thought it a nice perk to accompany the dinner blessing.

Jake's callused palm imprinted itself upon Shelby's skin and her thoughts, too. This was to be her wedding dinner. *Her wedding night.* And here she sat with a sweet dotty old saint who thought she was family and a stranger with a foreign touch.

Jake began passing dishes her way, giving her hands something useful to do and her thoughts a safe place to light. The chicken was moist and tender, the potatoes delicious and the sliced tomatoes, wonderful.

"Did you remember crochet thread, Wendy?" asked Gram Kate, looking at Shelby.

Shelby paused, fork in hand and lifted her eyes to Jake.

He smiled reassuringly and said, "I'll put it on the list, Gram."

"Thank you, dear. Have another biscuit. It's my special reci— Tea. More tea? You must have another piece of chicken, you're a growing boy."

Gram Kate passed everything Jake's way. He set the tea pitcher and the serving dishes to the center of the table, but she kept returning them to him. At length, he transferred the dishes to the counter.

"I'll wash," offered Shelby, coming to her feet.

"No need. I'll put them in the dishwasher later after we've had coffee," Jake replied and waved her down again.

Shelby was nursing a second cup when Paula and Joy let themselves in the back door. Paula was carrying a chocolate cake. Joy bumped Jake's chair and held out her hand.

"You owe me for fifty-seven weeds, Uncle Jake."

"She has been paid. Don't even think about it," Paula warned, as Jake reached for his wallet.

"Fifty-seven cents. You call that pay?" complained Joy.

Jake fished a five from his wallet.

"I mean it, Jake," Paula asserted.

"It isn't for weeding, it's a consulting fee. This is

Shelby Taylor. Shelby, my niece, Joy and my sister, Paula.''

Paula exchanged smiles with Shelby. ''We met earlier.''

''I heard Uncle Jake wrecked your car,'' Joy said, a lively interest in eyes a shade darker than Jake's.

''Her laptop was in the front seat. Seems to have suffered some injuries. It's upstairs in the guest room,'' Jake said. ''Take a look, would you?''

''I'll go with you.'' Shelby thanked Jake for the meal, excused herself, and followed Joy up the stairs.

Jake loaded the dishwasher, left Gram in Paula's capable hands, and joined them there.

''Any luck?'' he asked.

''Not yet,'' Joy replied. She poked keys in a free-wheeling frenzy.

Shelby stood by looking on, lip caught, expression apprehensive.

''Relax,'' soothed Jake. ''Blondie's a regular computer chip.''

''Not tonight, Uncle Jake. I can't get this thing to chirp.'' Joy glanced at Shelby, ''Sorry, Miss Taylor.''

''Please call me Shelby,'' said Shelby. ''I appreciate your efforts.''

''Me, too,'' chimed Jake. ''Thanks, sport.''

''It sure pays better than weeding your garden.'' Joy tugged the wrinkled five-dollar bill from her pocket and gave it a snap.

''Any word from Mr. Wiseman?'' Jake asked.

''Not yet. We drove by his house on the way over. His van is there, but no one answers the door.''

''Joy got a job cutting weeds out of soybean fields. But her boss seems to be lost,'' Jake explained.

"He owes us for sixty hours," Joy said. "Dirk's steamed."

"Who's Dirk?" asked Shelby.

"One of the guys on the crew. He's betting we've seen the last of Mr. Wiseman. Gave me a funny feeling right here," admitted Joy, hand on her midriff.

"You sure it isn't chocolate cake weighing you down?" teased Jake.

Joy twisted in her chair and tilted her chin toward Jake. "Did you try it?"

"Not yet."

"Chocolate's your favorite, right?" she asked.

"Second only to lemon chiffon," he claimed.

"Last time I baked cherry chip, and you said it was your favorite second only to chocolate," Joy reminded him.

"That so?" Jake grinned and said, "How about you, Shelby? You ready for dessert?"

"Maybe later. I'd like to work a while."

"I have a computer downstairs. You're welcome to use it," Jake offered, seeing Shelby reach for her tablet.

"You wouldn't mind?"

"Not at all," Jake answered. "I'm not up to speed on it, yet. But if you have any questions, Joy can help you out."

"Sure. Come on. I'll get you started," agreed Joy.

The word processing program was strikingly similar to Shelby's. With Joy's help, she soon had the basics down well enough to work.

"Keep it, Uncle Jake already paid me," Joy reminded, when Shelby tried to pay her for showing her the ropes.

"I want you to have it," Shelby insisted. "Please? It'll free me to ask again, should I need more help."

"All right then." She thanked Shelby, tucked the money into her pocket, and ventured in the same breath, "Winny Penn's mom says you were supposed to get married this weekend. So did you change your mind or what?"

Chapter Four

$\smile$

Jake walked through the garden, then moved the lawn sprinkler close enough to give the tomato plants a good drink. He glanced toward his lighted office window and returned to the porch to take off his damp boots. Paula joined him on the steps.

"Gram's tucked in," she offered. "Her eyes were closed almost before her head hit the pillow. What's this about your houseguest getting left at the altar?"

"Who told you *that?*" Jake asked, sitting straighter.

"Antoinette. I saw her at the store, and mentioned that you and Gram had a guest. It put her mind at ease to hear it. She felt terrible over having to turn Shelby away." Paula slid him a glance and ventured, "How's she holding up, anyway?"

"Couldn't say," he replied evenly.

Paula's gaze lingered, but she let the subject drop.

Dusk fell over the yard in deepening shades of purple. The shadows brought to Jake's mind the bruise of broken promises that lingered in Shelby's eyes. She was having a hard time of it, yet she didn't complain. There was nothing of the pathetic about her. He liked that. Liked her manner, too, how she had taken Gram's mental lapses into stride without comment.

Paula spoke up, asking about Joy's employer, Mr. Wiseman. "What do you suppose happened to him, anyway?"

"He'll turn up," Jake said.

"It is peculiar, though. And speaking of peculiar, what's this about you driving Joy to the edge of town to check out Colton's face-lift?"

"You mean the sign? That wasn't *my* idea," Jake answered.

"I guessed as much." Paula sighed. "She asks about him all the time lately. She can't understand why I never told him about her. She badgered me until I finally told her that as far as I'm concerned, Colt wouldn't be in the dark about her if he had stayed home where he belonged. It's the truth," she added.

Part of it, anyway. Calling the rest to mind served no purpose. Jake asked, "What'd she say?"

"'Get over it, Mom.'"

"She's just testing the stretch in your apron strings," Jake said. "You're doing just fine. Blondie's a good kid."

"By the grace of God and a lot of help from you." Paula patted his knee and came to her feet.

"Where you going?" asked Jake.

"Home. Joy's a bear to get up if she isn't in bed by ten."

"I'll get her for you," Jake offered.

"Thanks, Jake. I'll see you at church tomorrow." Paula crossed the yard to her car.

Jake dropped his boots inside the door and trekked through the house in his sock feet. The door to his office was open, the desk in full view. Joy and Shelby were side by side at his desk, facing the door. The computer monitor partially hid their faces.

"So how come he walked out on you?" he overheard Joy ask Shelby.

"He had his reasons," replied Shelby.

"Good ones?" pressed Joy.

"I suppose they were to him." Shelby glanced away from the computer screen and saw Jake. Dusky eyelids fell behind the lenses of her reading glasses. Color swept up her pale cheeks.

Jake's gut clenched at the humiliation in her swiftly averted gaze. "Your mom's waiting in the car," he said to Joy.

"But I'm showing Shelby how to…"

He cut her short. "I'll show her."

"Retrieve from the trash? You don't even know yourself, I'll bet," replied Joy, tipping her chin.

"Go home," he said.

"I was *trying* to help," she huffed.

"Some help," Jake muttered as Joy passed him in the door.

Joy made a face at him. He crossed to the desk, wondering whether to apologize to Shelby on Joy's behalf or pretend he hadn't overheard. He was opting for pretense when Joy called to him from the open door.

He pivoted to see her hand over the light switch.

"Nighty-night," she said as the room went dark.

"Turn it on, Joy," ordered Jake.

She snickered instead and closed the door behind her.

"Sorry, I don't know what gets into her," apologized Jake, though under the circumstances, darkness wasn't all that unwelcome.

"I gather she heard things," Shelby said.

"Not from me," he said quickly. "There's a remote switch. Reach into the desk drawer."

"Which drawer?"

"Top," Jake replied, though he could have as easily crossed to the switch. The drawer squeaked as she opened it. He heard pencils rub pencils, the metallic sift of paper clips and other desk drawer contents shift beneath Shelby's unseen fingers. The darkness amplified the cat-paw soft sounds of her search. That, and the silence to which Joy's cheeky question clung like a fly caught on a glue strip. No use ignoring it.

"I'll tell Paula to talk to her," he began.

"Please don't," Shelby interjected. "You've done enough."

Jake twitched, certain she believed him the source of the *things* that had piqued Joy's curiosity.

He circled the desk. "Slide back. I can put my hand right on it." In the absence of light, he misjudged her position. His hand skimmed her curls in a chance touch that tickled his palm and his fancy, too. "Sorry."

"My fault," Shelby murmured and rolled the desk chair away from the desk, giving him more room.

The darkness heightened her flower-sweet fragrance. Feeling enveloped by it, Jake's hand closed over the remote in the drawer. "Those your toes I'm walking on?" he asked, in no hurry to shed light on the room or the inspiration behind an unorthodox and not-so-chance but gentle collision of feet.

"No harm done," she said, and withdrew them.

Jake's sock-clad feet begged to disagree. The harm was a sweet ache that started in his feet the moment she pulled hers away. Jake swallowed a sigh and hit the remote. Light flooded the room. Her silk-stocking clad feet were tucked beneath the chair. He reached to close the yawning desk drawer and in so doing, noticed her shoes neatly aligned beneath his desk. They looked good there. Like small white hens come home to roost. Foolish to think it, much less want to say so. He moved to one side, making elbow room for her as she put on reading glasses, tilted the lined pad beside the keyboard and began typing.

"Ready for some cake now?" he asked for want of a better excuse to regain her attention.

"Thanks, but I'm not hungry."

Curious as what so firmly held her focus, Jake reached for her tablet. His finger barely touched down when she whisked it away. He blinked, cupped his elbow in one hand and rubbed his chin. "So, what's this you're writing?"

"Not much at the rate I'm going," she said, her fingers poised over the keyboard.

Jake leaned in, trying to read the screen. Her silky lashes swept upward, lush and long and thick. Strained patience flashed in hazel depths. "Sorry," he said, and backed away.

"For what?"

"Well, I don't know exactly. But I didn't get that much of a reaction when I dropped my crane on your car," he said, wincing.

Color flooded Shelby's face. Grabbing the tablet

was pure reflex. Just as strong was the urge to erase the screen with a keystroke rather than to let him read her work before it was finished and polished. Unwilling to admit how raw and inadequate her first drafts seemed to her, and how she cringed at the thought of anyone else reading them, she swept a curl behind her ear, and explained, "What I'm working on is a rough draft. If I let you read it, it weakens my motivation to finish the thing."

"Top secret, eh? Now I *am* intrigued."

"You have no hang-ups?" she countered quietly.

"Classified, like your story," he claimed.

His gentle jesting cooled her rising hackles and left a foolish grin on her face. She wiped it clean, curled a leg beneath her and offered, "Shall I have my publisher send you a copy?"

"Will you sign it for me?" he pressed, mouth tilting.

"If you like."

"Just your name? Or could I have an inscription, too? Something like, 'To Jake, You Have My Number.'"

"I sure do," she countered.

He laughed and she smiled and the anchor eased its grip on her heart. But only for a moment. The interest flickering in his eyes reminded her that Patrick had once looked at her that way, too. Rejection, like honeybees, left the stinger in. Shelby averted her face before the heat of that bite brushed her cheeks.

"What's it take?" asked Jake. At her blank glance, he propped a hip on the corner of the desk and added, "Time wise, I mean."

"From here to here in a year." She tapped her

temple, then spread her hands as if she held a book. "Unless I get stuck."

"I better go then, and let you get back to it," said Jake.

Her smile, though fleeting, did nice things to her face. Like the blush on a peach. Though on closer scrutiny, Jake found that pinch never quite left her eyes. Her lashes came down, closing the beaches on those hazel seas. Intrigued, he wondered at her thoughts. That, at least was rational. The impulse to sweep her out of her chair and into his arms to kiss those pinch lines into retreat was not.

"I'll see you in the morning," he said, and came to his feet.

"Good night. Thanks for everything," she called, breathing easier now that he was leaving.

Jake wished she would use his name. He hesitated a moment, realizing he hadn't used hers, either. It formed on his tongue. But already, she had shut him out. Her white fingers were over the keys, skipping like whitecaps. Divorce, Jake had heard, was second only in trauma to suffering the death of a loved one. Where, then, did getting jilted rank? Somewhere in the ballpark with desertion, he wagered. He was still seeing the consequences of that in Paula's life, and Joy's too, as she struggled to fill the void left by a father who didn't know she existed.

Jake checked on Gram before turning in. It was a long while later when he heard water running and knew Shelby had called it quits for the night. He rubbed one eye and peered at the illuminated dial of his alarm clock. It was 3:00 a.m. And after the day she had had. She had stamina.

Jake rolled over and slept until the aroma of perking coffee stirred him awake. It was six. He could have grabbed another hour of sleep. But these days, Gram and the stove were an unpredictable mix.

Shelby smelled coffee and heard voices. In the time it took her to get her bearings, she remembered she had no car, and nowhere she had to be today. On that note, she dozed off again and got up a good while later to an empty house. A shower and a dash of lipstick helped a face in need of some color. She rubbed scented hand cream from elbows to fingertips and went downstairs.

There was coffee in a carafe and cold bacon and biscuits on the kitchen table. Shelby made a biscuit sandwich and poured coffee. She ate quickly, carried her dishes to the sink, turned on the tap and her thoughts, too. By the time she reached the study, words were crowding, wanting out.

Ringing church bells drew Shelby to the window at noon. Moments later, Jake's Jeep turned up the back alley and parked in the drive alongside his building. He climbed out loosening his tie and circled to help Gram Kate from the front seat. Three more cars pulled in behind him. Doors flew open and a blend of Jacksons piled out. Shelby assumed they were Jacksons—lanky frames and blue eyes were in the majority. She watched Joy turn down the alley. A boy pedaled toward her on his bicycle. Joy hurried to meet him. They slipped out of sight behind Jake's sign building.

Jake climbed the stairs to change out of his suit and saw the guest room was empty. He returned downstairs and found Shelby at his desk. Her fingers moved over the keys. She paused, lips pursed, and typed on, unaware of him in the open door. It was the sort of concentration he looked for in crane operators. He could have used some of it himself yesterday on the bank building, letting his eye stray to a pretty woman climbing out of her car in the lot below. For all the good it did. It was plain to see that her heart was still attached to the one who had cut her free.

Smitten in spite of himself, he called to her, "How's the story coming?"

She glanced away from the screen. "Pretty well, thank you."

"Doesn't seem like much of a vacation, closed in with your work."

"It's a treat not to have to squeeze it in between my hours at the office." She pushed her chair back, and rose smoothing her dress. It was sleeveless, with a fitted yoke, brown as toast. A drift of yellow pleats fell from the bodice.

"That's a nice sunflower dress you're wearing," said Jake, though the loose fit left a lot to the imagination.

"And you said you didn't know flowers," she countered.

Jake grinned. "No, but I've pulled enough weeds..."

"It's a weed? A sunflower is a weed?" she said doubtfully. "Are you sure?"

"Look it up." Jake reached for his favorite gardening book on the desk, and pushed it her way.

Shelby thumbed through dog-eared pages and plunked back into her chair. "You're right."

His mouth tipped at her disheartened sigh. "I haven't ruined it for you, have I?"

"'A rose by any other name'..." She set the quote adrift, and tucked a curl behind her ear. The pencil tunneled there wobbled and fell in her lap. "How was church?"

"Crowded," he replied, and ducked under the desk to retrieve the pencil. "But we would have made room for you."

"I overslept. By the way, I've been thinking about that loaner car. Perhaps it's time I phoned *my* insurer."

"No use trying on Sunday," he told her, fingers brushing hers as he returned the pencil. Her nails were trimmed short, but neatly curved and tinted ivory. "Anyway, I checked with my agent last night. He said he would have a car for you sometime tomorrow."

"Fine," Shelby said. "I'll stop by your shop then, and get the manuscripts out of the trunk."

"If they're that important, we can go today," he offered.

"Could we? I wouldn't bother you with it, but I'm responsible for them," she explained.

"We'll go after lunch. My sisters brought covered dishes for lunch," he said.

"What can I do to help?"

"You're a glutton for punishment, aren't you?"

She smiled and followed him into the kitchen where he made introductions, then slipped upstairs to change out of his suit.

There was enough physical similarity between Jake's sisters that Shelby had a hard time remembering who was who. It was even more difficult with the children. Shelby counted seven boys and six girls. Then Joy came dashing in, flushed and fresh as a rosebud dressed all in pink.

"Where you been?" asked one of her cousins.

Joy pinched his arm.

"Ouch!" he squealed. "Quit it, Blondie Blake-a-cake."

Joy's giggly cousins shouted with laughter and took up the chant: "Blondie Blake-a-cake! Blondie bake-a-cake, Blake-a-cake,"

"You better quit calling me that or you won't be eating any of *my* cake," warned Joy with a lofty sniff.

"Another cake? You're turning into a regular Sara Lee," Jake said, joining the teasing.

He had changed into khakis and a loose-fitting shirt that suited his eyes. The writer in Shelby made mental notes. Preoccupied with the process, she saw his smile shift to silent inquiry and realized her gaze had lingered too long. His smile came on again as their eyes met. The glow of it spread heat within, like bottled sunshine. Startled at her instinctive response, Shelby averted her glance and finished setting the table. When the dinner call came, Jake held a chair for her, another for Joy, and settled between them.

The family joined hands for the blessing. Once again, Shelby found herself comparing Jake's broad, callused palm to the one her heart knew so well. With an effort, she focused on the bountiful table and the congeniality of Jake's family. The adults were welcoming, the children boisterous and lively. The meal, right through to dessert, was seasoned with humor and affection, and a balm to Shelby's bruised spirits.

"Scratch chocolate. Lemon's my favorite," Jake told Joy as he dribbled warm lemon sauce over his slice of lemon cake. "Second only to butter bean."

"Butter bean? I never heard of butter bean cake," said Joy.

Everyone laughed.

Joy's cheeks turned as pink as her dress. "You made that up," she accused, and flipped her braid over her shoulder.

"It's served in all the finest restaurants," claimed Jake. "A real delicacy. Isn't that right, Shelby?" he prompted with a gentle elbow and a blue-eyed wink.

Shelby indicated her mouth was too full to answer.

Thwarted, Jake wagged his head. "And here we were about to cut you in on our after-dinner baseball game."

The children gulped dessert, grabbed their baseball gloves and tramped out, arguing over teams. The men followed. Shelby stayed behind with Jake's sisters to clear away dinner and learned how to load and start the dishwasher.

Afterward Paula, Wendy and Jake's other sisters joined Gram Kate on the veranda. Shelby slipped up to her room for her notebook. She was on her way down to the study when Jake met her on the stairs.

"You're not going to spend your afternoon working, surely," he chided.

"I'm behind," she explained.

"Good position to be in." Grinning, he pivoted on the step. "You won't go wrong. Fall in behind me, and I'll take you out for some air."

"I meant behind on my work," she protested.

"Even God rested from His work on the seventh day."

His plainspoken logic nudged Shelby's conscience. But it was his coaxing smile that tipped the scales. "You're right, you know." Capitulating, she followed him downstairs.

"You want to pitch?" he asked on the way outdoors.

"No, thanks. Words are the only game I have any success with. Anyway, I'm resting. Remember?"

Jake chuckled at having his own words fed back to him. He left her with his sisters, and joined his team of Jackson progeny waiting in the yard. Shelby shaded her eyes and watched from a wicker lounger a makeshift game of men and kids and elastic rules that stretched to accommodate the smallest among them.

"So tell us, Shelby. What is it you're writing about?" asked Jake's youngest sister, Wendy.

"Teens," Shelby said.

"Joy's twelve, and already, I feel like *I* could do a book on teens!" exclaimed Paula.

In the company of her sisters, Paula was just one talker among many. Shelby's gaze returned to the game, and Jake, now hunkered down behind home plate with a catcher's mitt in hand.

"Hey, batter, batter," he chanted as a young nephew toddled up to bat. After the second strike, Jake dropped his glove and helped the pint-size batter swing.

The little guy was stunned when the bat cracked the ball. "Jimmy hit!" he cried. "Jimmy hit!"

"Run, Jimmy! Run!" hollered Jimmy's father, Curtis.

Jimmy froze, clutching the bat. Jake scooped him up and ran the bases with him. Jimmy was still clinging to the bat when they crossed home plate. He beamed as Jake set him down amidst his cheering teammates.

"Jimmy hit," he said again.

"Jimmy sure did!" Jake heaved Jimmy aloft and onto his shoulder and ran a victory lap.

"Jake needs a family of his own," Wendy commented.

"Wendy hasn't been married long," Paula said to Shelby. "The blush is still on the rose."

"But the kids do love Jake," pointed out Jimmy's mom, Christine. "Joy thinks the sun rises and sets on him."

"She should. He's always been there for us," Paula stated.

"That's all good and well. But it's time he was thinking about a nest of his own." Wendy turned a beaming smile on Shelby. "Say! Do you have any friends we could set him up with?"

"I could probably think of someone. But it would be a long drive for him," Shelby replied, rising from her chair. She caught Paula rolling her eyes, and angled for the door, adding, "Excuse me, would you? I left my sunglasses upstairs."

"That was real subtle, Wen," Paula chided Wendy.

"What?" protested Wendy with feigned innocence. "All I said was, did she know anyone."

Restless, Shelby retrieved her sunglasses, and on impulse, phoned her parents. No one answered. She wasn't surprised. They were very busy. Even in childhood, it was a catch-as-catch-can proposition.

She left a message explaining the circumstances that had forced a change of plans, where she was staying and how to reach her. As she did so, she could almost see them trading benign and somewhat surprised glances at her bid to reassure them she was fine. It wouldn't occur to them to think otherwise.

Ball game forgotten, Shelby let herself into Jake's study, closed the door and turned on the computer. Time fell away as she polished her first chapter.

THE FIELD
Chapter One

The sun was rising as Cheryl gathered with half a dozen sleepy-eyed teens beneath the park pavilion. Yesterday's rain had distorted the bill of her Weed Buster's cap. Her sneakers were stiff with dried mud and the edges of her cutoff shorts were unraveling.

"So where's the boss?" she asked one of the boys waiting there.

"Who cares? he said. "Waiting's easy cash."

Cheryl wished she could be so carefree. She looked up the empty street, then sat down on a picnic table to wait. As the minutes stretched into half an hour with no sign of Mr. Weedman, the rest of the kids picked up their lunches and hoes and ambled away, Dudley among them.

But Cheryl stayed, pacing now. He would be along anytime with a logical explanation. He would apologize for keeping her waiting. They would round up the other kids and go to the field.

Seven-thirty and still no Weedman. Where was he? Why didn't he come? She needed to work. Needed the money. Needed to kill weeds and self-doubts. Blue-eyed dirt-track speed-demon Jack Cook, in not exposing her, had given her purpose. She wanted to be who he thought she could be.

Seven forty-five. Get a brain, Cheryl. He isn't coming! She picked up her lunch cooler, her hoe. And yet…what harm was there in waiting a few more minutes?

Eight o'clock. No Weedman. Cheryl was angry now. And scared. She tried to reason away the fear. But she was cold inside. Cold with the growing conviction that something was terribly wrong. That she had seen the last of Wiley Weedman.

And she was dead right.

"So here you are! Why aren't I surprised?"

Shelby looked to find Jake leaning in the door, a grass stain on one knee of his khakis and his baseball cap in hand. "Who won?" she asked, her eyes returning to the screen.

"Hard to say when it erupts into a brawl," he said. "I called the game. Gram separated them as best she could, put them in their cars and sent them home."

"Hmm," Shelby replied, struggling against the gravitational pull of her story.

"It tuckered her out, until it was all she could do to climb in the last car out the drive. She said don't wait supper, she'll make them feed her before she comes home." Jake crossed to the window and lowered the blinds. "If you can find a stopping place there, we'll go into town and rescue your homework. May as well eat while we're at it."

"Is it that time already?"

"Getting close," he said. "If you're not hungry, we could go for a walk."

"After an afternoon of baseball?" Trying to talk words at odds with the words she was typing was too much. Shelby looked up just as Jake perched on the corner of the desk and reached for her hand-scrawled notes.

"Please don't..."

"...read your stuff," he finished, withholding the tablet.

Shelby restrained herself from leaping across the desk and wrestling her tablet away. His baiting smile triggered heat, which she strove to hide, even as she tried to divert his attention from her scribbled notes. "About this walk. Would it take us past Mr. Wiseman's house?" she asked.

"I guess it could. Why?"

Shelby hit a key, watched the screen darken and pushed out of her chair. "Has he turned up yet?"

"Not that I know of," Jake said.

"Do I have time to run upstairs and get my walking shoes?"

"Sure. No hurry. Aren't you forgetting something?" he called after her.

Shelby turned in the door and caught the tablet as he pitched it across the room. "You're a tease, Jake."

He crooked a brow and countered, "Here I thought you had eyes only for your story."

"You noticed?"

"That you weren't hanging on my every word? Of course I noticed. What man wouldn't?"

He spoke in jest. And still it gave Shelby pause, for until that moment, it hadn't occurred to her that anyone but Patrick would find her preoccupation with her story objectionable. She mulled the thought as she climbed the stairs to freshen up. What good was a forward view if her future became a repeat of the same conflict she had had with Patrick? Hearing the phone ring, Shelby tucked away the thought with her tablet, splashed her face and combed her hair and returned downstairs.

"I thought she left with you," she heard Jake say as she joined him in the living room. "No, she's not here. Sure, I'll send a carton with her if she turns up."

"Who's missing?" Shelby asked.

"Joy. She told her mom she would walk home. Paula thought maybe she could catch her before she left. She's out of eggs." He held the door for Shelby.

The air had cooled. It was fragrant with the neighbor's freshly clipped grass and pine needles. A canopy of old trees shaded the crumbling sidewalk.

"Liberty Flats," murmured Shelby when the silence grew heavy. "Kind of an odd name for rolling prairie, isn't it?"

"I guess it is if you don't know its story," Jake replied. "The township was settled by abolitionist farmers from the east. Along with forty acres of land, each settler got a lot in a little town they called Liberty. Some men in the colony ran a station on the underground railroad. Thus, the name."

Shelby listened as he explained that when the railroad bypassed Liberty a few years before the Civil

War, the tiny village was doomed to return to the prairie.

"A guy by the name of Dan Flats came along and offered to sell the town fathers some land adjacent to the tracks, if they wanted to pull up stakes and relocate Liberty. He quoted a bargain rate with the stipulation that they name the new town for him," Jake continued. "So when the ground was frozen, Liberty loaded their houses and sheds onto ox-driven sleds and moved east three miles. And Liberty Flats was born,"

"Interesting stuff," Shelby said, silently appraising the easy pride he took in his hometown.

"It gets better," Jake continued. "A few years went by, and come to find out Flats didn't have clear title on the land he had sold. The public was put out enough at dapper Dan, they tried to change the town name."

"To what?"

"That was the problem. They couldn't agree. By then, Dan's grown sons had put down roots in town. When it came to a vote, Liberty Flats got seven votes. The rest were split between a dozen other suggestions. So Liberty Flats carried the day," explained Jake. "Dan was pleased enough, he nailed together a little hotel by the railroad tracks, and spent the rest of his life in Liberty Flats, trying to clear himself of any wrongdoing. Claimed he'd been taken in by a slick land agent."

"Was that true?"

"According to Dan's descendants, it is," Jake said. But his grin left room for doubt.

Modern concrete gave way to quaint brick sidewalk. Flower beds dotted green lawns that unfolded toward the street. Jake paused beside a picket fence. "This is it. Wilt Wiseman's place."

Shelby stopped in front of the two-story clapboard of chipping paint and fading glory. The grass needed cutting, the newspapers were piling up and a garbage can at the back corner of the house was overflowing.

Shelby was about to walk on when she heard a clatter. Joy, still clad in her pink dress, darted into view without seeing them. She grabbed the garbage can by one handle and dragged it behind the house.

"Now what do you suppose *she's* up to?" Jake opened the gate, took a beaten path skirting the house and disappeared around the far corner.

Chapter Five

Shelby's nerves leapt as a young man came racing from the far side of the house. He was a dead ringer for the boy she had seen at noon in the alley by Jake's sign building. As she stood watching, he jerked a bicycle out from beneath a bush, pedaled through the open gate, and tore down the street. A moment later, Jake returned with Joy, whining and dragging her feet.

"I suppose you're gonna tell Mom."

"No," said Jake, jaw clenched. "*You* are. If I hadn't come along when I did, you'd have been through that window."

"I was just trying to figure out what happened to Mr. Wiseman," defended Joy. "What if he's lying in there sick or hurt, and nobody checks on him? I keep telling you I have a funny feeling about him."

"I have a funny feeling, too. Says you had some help here," replied Jake. "And I *don't* mean a garbage can for a stepladder."

Joy's gaze skipped over the bush that had only a moment ago concealed a bicycle.

"You want to tell me who talked you into doing something so irresponsible?" Jake pressed.

"Nobody," Joy said, sulking.

"Come on, Joy. Level with me. Was it Dirk?"

"You're not my dad, I don't have to tell you anything," Joy huffed. She swung around with her chin set and stormed away.

"Dirk, or I miss my guess," Jake muttered, watching her flounce down the street.

"You saw him?" Shelby asked.

"After church," Jake said. "He followed us home on his bike."

"He was here a minute ago," Shelby informed Jake. "He tore away while you were in back. Is he prone to trouble?"

"Not that I know of. Though crawling through Mr. Wiseman's kitchen window is a sure invitation for it," Jake added.

"Granted, it was a poor judgment call. But their motives were understandable," Shelby reasoned.

"I should hope," Jake said, relenting a little. He turned back the way they had come.

Shelby started to follow, then stopped and looked back. "What if they're right, Jake? What if Mr. Wiseman *is* inside alone, needing help? We could at least check with the neighbors, couldn't we?" Shelby persisted for peace of mind.

It didn't seem likely to Jake. But to be on the safe side, he checked with the next-door neighbor, who had a key to the Wiseman house. The neighbor, Roxelle, let herself into the house, and came out a moment later to say there was no one inside.

"Mrs. Wiseman works for a genealogical research firm," Roxelle explained. "Sometimes, Mr. Wiseman helps her with the research. Especially when it takes her out of town."

"That must be what happened," Jake agreed.

"I'll have them call Joy when they arrive home," the neighbor promised.

Jake thanked her for her trouble. He and Shelby walked home where Jake showered and changed for their dinner date. They took the interstate to a fifties-style diner at the south edge of Bloomington. Inside, neon, classic car posters and photos of movie stars from that era brightened the walls. Jake emptied his change into a jukebox. He and Shelby poured over a collection of oldies, making selections, and then studied the menu while pop country entertainers crooned the blues.

"Paula did the neon for this place," Jake told Shelby.

"It's very nice," Shelby said. She hesitated a moment. "Forgive my curiosity, but I've been wondering about Joy's father."

"Colton? I take it Joy mentioned the billboard," Jake responded.

"Billboard?" she echoed.

"The Voyager." Belatedly, Jake saw he had jumped to conclusions, that she didn't know about Joy's father after all. "Colton did some modeling for Wind, Water and Sky. It was the beginning of an ad campaign that has since given him nationwide recognition."

"I'm sorry, I'm not following you," Shelby said, struggling to make the connection between a billboard and Joy's father.

"That's Colt," Jake told her.

"The Voyager? The guy in the canoe wearing the red cap? You don't mean it!" cried Shelby.

"One and the same," Jake said, as amazement lighted her eyes.

"The Voyager! I can't believe it! Why, he's a household word, and has been for years. And he's Joy's father! How on earth did he and Paula meet?"

"Colt came to Liberty Flats as a investigative journalist, looking into a train derailing and a nasty chemical spill that hadn't been properly cleaned up," Jake explained.

"A writer, too. I had no idea," Shelby murmured, pleased to learn that there was more to the man than rugged handsomeness. "How long did he live in Liberty Flats?"

"He didn't. He was here just three weeks getting the details for his report and romancing Paula. He returned a few weeks later and they were married. It didn't last long. The day Colt left, Paula was sick in bed in their Chicago flat with what she thought was the flu. By the time she realized it was morning sickness, she had moved back home, and Colt was out of her life for good."

"Why would he have such a change of heart?" Shelby asked, her heart hurting for Paula.

The answer lay on a dark rainy road strewn with premature loss and memories that remained painful even with the passage of time. Reluctant to go there, Jake was relieved when the waitress arrived to take their orders.

When she had gone, he guided the conversation down less treacherous paths, asking Shelby about her former books, the titles, the content, the message. A light came on in her eyes as she spoke of those things. Jake smiled as she confided that she found Joy to be interesting story inspiration.

"Do us a favor, and don't tell her," he quipped. "It'll go straight to her head, and there'll be no living with her."

Shelby smiled and cleared up his misconception, saying, "The book isn't *about* her. By inspiration, I mean Joy freshens in me the angst, the dreams, the pressures of those teen years."

"Oh, that! Terrific! Glad to hear someone's getting some good out of her mood swings. She's giving Paula anxiety attacks."

"And her uncle?"

Jake grinned at her shrewdness. "She's a good kid. Other than your occasional break and entry."

They lingered over coffee and conversation. It was dusk by the time they arrived at Jackson Signs to retrieve Shelby's book bag from the trunk of her demolished car.

"If my insurance agent doesn't come through with that loaner tomorrow, you're welcome to use the Jeep," Jake told Shelby as they climbed out of his vehicle.

"That won't be necessary," Shelby said. "I'll spend the day writing. Or will you be needing your computer?"

"No problem. I have access at both shops," Jake assured her. He paused beneath a vapor light and plucked a crowbar from the toolbox of a crane truck. "How much vacation time do you have?"

"A week," Shelby replied. "But I'll get out of your way just as soon as I get a car."

"You're not in my way. Gram's enjoying having another woman in the house," said Jake.

"She thinks I'm your sister."

"That bothers you?"

"No, of course not. She's very sweet," Shelby amended hastily.

Jake slapped a mosquito and fell silent as they closed the distance to her battered car. An apology hovered on Shelby's tongue. But the moment was lost to the shriek of metal as Jake, crowbar in hand, pried at the stubborn trunk lid.

"I'm sorry, Jake," Shelby said quietly, when he paused to wipe his glistening face and calibrate his progress.

"For what?" His eyes met hers and tinged the dusky light.

Shelby lost her courage in that haze of midnight blue. "I didn't realize it would be such a job."

"It's me. I'm making uphill work of it." He slapped and bloodied another mosquito. "I'll open the shop and get the handyman jack."

Upon his return with the jack, Shelby got a glimpse of his face as he passed beneath the vapor light. *He's forgotten it. Let it go.* She trained a curl behind her ear, and stood by as Jake secured the jack. It didn't take him long to pop open the trunk. Shelby dived past him and scooped up her book bag.

"Safe and sound?" he asked, thinking what a waste it was, those slim arms hugging soulless tapestry and paper.

Shelby checked inside. "Seems to be."

"Good. I'll lock up and we'll get going, before the mosquitoes eat us alive," he stated, and strode away, whistling off-key, his cap askew and the heavy jack slung over his shoulder.

On the ride home, Shelby said no more about leaving. That pleased Jake. The truth was, everything about her pleased him. Her shining curls and hazel eyes. Her mannerisms. The notice she took of the smallest kindness.

While her remark concerning Gram's forgetfulness had caught him off guard, on further reflection, he appreciated her honesty. Some folks pretended not to notice Gram Kate's confusion while other well-meaning friends didn't understand the family effort to keep Gram in her own home.

"A few weeks, and she wouldn't know the difference," a neighbor had said not long ago.

Maybe not. But he would and his sisters would, too.

Wendy turned into the driveway just ahead of them and let Gram Kate out. Gram said her goodbyes. She linked arms with Jake and Shelby and strolled to the house between them. "Let's have some tea and toast," she said.

In no hurry to see the evening end, Jake smiled at Shelby, bidding her to join them. "What's your pleasure, whole wheat or sourdough?" he asked.

"Whole wheat. Point me in the right direction, and I'll help," she offered.

"It's my treat, dear," Gram responded. She padded from the kitchen sink to the stove with the teapot. "How was the picture sho-sho-shoot?"

"We didn't go to the show. But we had a nice dinner," Shelby said.

"This finicky old fussbudget," grumbled Gram

Kate when the burner failed to light. "Where did I put the matches?"

"Gram, you don't need a match." Jake stepped in. "The stove is new, remember? Just turn it to 'light.'"

"The tin, of course." Struggling to open the match tin, Gram missed Jake's demonstration of how to operate the stove. "Empty," she muttered, frustration creeping into her voice.

"It's real simple, Gram Kate. Look. Like this." Jake took the empty tin. He showed her the light indicator on the burner knob and indicated the clicking sound that began when the burner lit. "Adjust the flame and the clicking stops."

"Fuss and nonsense," grumbled Gram. Toast and tea forgotten, she ambled off, muttering to herself.

Jake met Shelby's sympathetic glance. "So much for electric ignition. Matches, she understood."

"But of course," Shelby said. "Where else do you get such instantaneous results?"

"Women." Jake wagged his head and turned up his palms with an engaging grin. "*I'll* make the tea. You man the toaster, and stay away from the matches."

Shelby chuckled and reached into the bread box.

It was a big kitchen, but it closed in nicely as they shared counter space and a simple task. Jake held the door leading out to the summer porch where Gram had settled. Shelby brushed by him, tea tray in hand. The ceiling fan hummed lazily overhead, blending fragrances—dew-drenched flowers, green grass, sweet clover and the apple blossom scent Shelby was wearing.

A yellow tabby begged from the porch steps.

Gram swung the screen door open and let the cat in. "There, there, Kitty," she soothed the cat's plaintive meow with a toast crust dipped in cream. When the treat was gone, Kitty groomed and preened, then played a game of cat and mouse with a moth.

Shelby took pity and released the moth outdoors. She refilled Gram's cup and her own cup, too.

"No, thanks." Jake declined, covering the rim of his cup with his hand.

Shelby wandered to the edge of the porch with her cup and saucer in hand. Jake admired the pretty silhouette she made. He joined her there, enjoying the dark air, the shadows and placid sounds of night settling in.

Fireflies danced and a new moon climbed the sky. Kitty purred from pillar to post, arching her back against Shelby's shapely ankle, then weaving a path between Jake's spread feet. He stooped and stroked the cat's ears, then let her out to prowl the summer night.

Gram yawned and came to her feet. "You have school tomorrow, Jill. Ten minu—men you mend, say good—good…" she sighed and gave up getting the words out and kissed Shelby's cheek. She kissed Jake, too, and went inside.

Shelby slipped into the chair Gram had vacated and brushed a loose thread from her skirt. "Who's Jill?" she asked quietly.

"My mother."

He glimpsed Shelby waiting, lips parted. When he offered nothing further, she busied herself clearing away. The clamor of clattering spoons and cups and the graceful hands that gathered them revealed a void in Jake he hadn't had the luxury to think about much lately. He moved to the porch swing, and patted the slatted seat.

"Let those go, and come sit a while."

Shelby swung around, her smile barely touching down.

"You're supposed to be on vacation," he reminded.

"I know. I think I'll work a while," she said, then grimaced at the inconsistency of her words, and laughed at herself.

Jake planted his feet, stopping the swing in wordless entreaty. She joined him there, her elbow finding rest on the wooden arm. She seemed more relaxed than she had a day ago. Yet on closer accounting, Jake saw that moonglow and cricket cadence hadn't erased the pinched expression from her eyes.

"Here's a penny for your thoughts," he offered.

Shelby touched the coin he fished from his pocket. "I was thinking about the unplanned turns in the line."

"What lines?" asked Jake.

"Life."

Jake turned her hand up. It was soft to the touch, pliant, yet firm. He traced a faint crease. "This one the lifeline?"

Her gaze fell to his hand holding her open palm and suddenly, levity vanished and pliancy too. "That isn't what I meant."

"What, then?" Jake released her hand before she could withdraw it.

She ducked her head. He thought she would duck the question, too. Instead, she murmured, "We were a year planning this weekend."

"So what gives with the guy?" Jake took the opening her words provided.

"His name is Patrick," she said in a hush.

Jake watched her fingers tighten around the supporting swing chain. "Patrick has a hard time making up his mind, does he?"

"Not as a rule," she said in the same careful voice. "He's an attorney and proficient at it. Analytical. Methodical. Nothing escapes him."

"You did."

"That was *his* choice."

"Suppose he does an about-face?" asked Jake.

"He won't. He said it was paramount to adultery."

"He's married?" blurted Jake, startled out of his feigned casual pursuit of her severed relationship.

"No. I am. To my writing, he says." Her attempted levity failed. Fatigue tugged at her eyes, painting shadows.

Jake stretched his arm across the back of the swing. He started to cup her shoulder, to commiserate with a pat and a word, but on further consideration, found his motives suspect, and thought better of it.

"Forgive me, I didn't mean to unload on you," she murmured at his silence.

"Get it out, if it helps."

"To bore you with it?"

"You couldn't if you tried."

"You're sweet," she said.

He could be a lot sweeter. Wanted to be. Her chin quivered, a brave effort at a smile that turned watery. He gripped splintered wood, countermanding the urge to gather her in. The porch lamp illuminated lines and traces beneath misty eyes and a fragile mouth. Moth wings brushed the glass lamp, soft as the breath she expelled.

"We'd been dating for two years before marriage came up. It took us another year to plan the perfect wedding," she confided. "Then a week ago, all that changed. I spent every spare moment returning gifts, calling guests, the florist, the caterer, the bakery. The only thing Patrick canceled was the one thing I was still counting on."

"The cottage at Wildwood?"

Shelby nodded.

"Deliberately?"

"No. Patrick isn't like that," she replied quickly. "It was lack of communication. He didn't know I had decided to go alone."

Her defense of the guy surprised Jake less than the sting it gave him. He fumbled his coin, wrestling with the realization she was just the kind of woman he'd like to have in his corner. The penny bounced to the floor and rolled into a puddle of light.

Shelby stopped it with her foot. "Next time I'm eloping," she said surprising a smile out of him. "No fuss, no bother,"

"That's right, climb right back into the saddle," he encouraged, finding his stride, heart soaring at the possibilities.

"You bet," she said.

Through a divide in the slatted swing, Jake stroked her back with the flat of his thumb. She retreated from his touch, leaning forward ostensibly to pick up the coin. Jake caught his breath, waiting.

"I didn't mean..." she began as she straightened.

"Course not," he said. He jammed the offending

thumb inside a curled fist and commiserated, saying, "Hurts, huh?"

She darted him a wary glance. "You've been there?"

"Not in the same way," he said. "But loss is loss."

"How did you weather it?"

"Not too well. It was my parents."

Jake heard her breath catch. "Both of them?" she asked.

"In a car accident. Paula's husband was driving the car that hit them," he said tonelessly, and saw her hand fly to her throat. "He wasn't seriously hurt. But it was a tough time for everyone."

Appalled at all Jake's family had suffered, and feeling her own troubles slight by comparison, Shelby murmured, "I'm so sorry, Jake."

Her eyes swelled with compassion, and the emotion caught him by the throat. The tightness of the grip got beyond his guard. He averted his gaze. A window closed across the street. A car turned around in the alley. Water dripped from the nearby faucet where the garden hose and the spigot met. He shifted to his feet to shut off the sprinkler. Time fell away and in spirit, he was that grown boy again. Coming home late, dodging the lawn sprinkler, wondering what Gram was doing at their house. He was that fly-apart boy, hearing the words and going to pieces. And Gram was herself again, her faith strong even in her weakest hour. She said of his parents, "'Jesus called in a trumpet voice, Come up here.'"

Later Jake had found those words in his Bible and understood better the tender concern behind them, and the power with which they were spoken. He couldn't verbalize what they had come to mean to him. Or why they were so strongly in mind as he reclaimed his place on the swing.

It was Shelby who moved closer. Her voice was softly plaintive. "Is it just a cliché, time heals?"

"Time doesn't just heal. It moves forward with a will and a purpose."

"On better days?" she said finally.

"On eternity."

Her eyes filled again. Too late, Jake saw that forever was a long time to be disconnected from a man she had loved and lost, not by death but by a change of heart. "It was a quote from something a friend sent to me after the funeral. I didn't understand it at the time," Jake admitted.

"And later?"

"It's the Spirit that gives life. Mom and Dad had already died to themselves years before when they said I do to God." Seeing her confusion, he murmured, "Their confession of faith."

"Oh, *that*," she said and closed her eyes, remembering a time when Patrick had had everything she wanted in a man, *except* faith. It was at Can-Do, a homeless mission where Shelby had talked him into volunteering several hours a week, that he came to know the Lord. In her eyes, that made him complete. But shared faith had not saved their relationship.

"I'm sorry," Jake murmured, his eyes seeming dark in the shadows. "I'm not much good at this."

"Yes, you are. You've helped." So saying, she tucked heart wounds beneath a veneered smile and tilted her chin. "No good sympathizing with myself. Onward and upward, as they say."

But for all her brave intentions, tears escaped and

coursed down her cheek. "Stop that." She mopped her cheek with the back of her hand and flashed a watery smile.

Jake offered his handkerchief.

"Feel better?" he asked, when she had dried her eyes.

"I'm going to, I promise." She returned his handkerchief and reached as if to touch him the way friends will. But at the last moment, her hand drifted back to her lap without making contact. "Thanks for listening. You've been an angel. Offering your home, your family, your hospitality. You're heaven sent," she insisted.

"To drop a crane on your car?"

She dried the last stray tear from her cheek with the back of her hand. "Perhaps I'll get a chance to return the kindness."

"No need. Really," he said and flung arms in the air as if ducking a falling crane.

Her smile jerked at his heart. Caught between laughter and an open flame, he curled his hand around the handkerchief, damp with her tears and got to his feet.

Together, they carried the cups and saucers and remnants of their snack inside. Together, they washed and wiped them dry. Together, they spoke of everyday things. The sign business. Her family. His. And mosquitoes. She rubbed one welt and then another. Jake had a dozen to match.

"There's ointment upstairs in the medicine cabinet that will take the sting away," he told her.

Wishing the cut of severed hearts could be so easily remedied, Shelby thanked him again, bid him good-night, and climbed the stairs.

Family portraits lined the landing walls between closed doors. Previously, she had given them only passing notice. Now, she searched faces and found Jake's parents among them, encircled by Jake's bevy of sisters. Paula, the eldest, glowing with happiness, no clue as to the heartache that lay ahead. And Jake, his hand on his mother's shoulder. Jake hadn't shared his family tragedy to minimize her loss. And yet it did. It dwarfed her childhood pangs, as well. She remembered once, questioning her mother for writing *Homemaker* as her occupation on a grant she was writing for one charity or another.

Confused, she'd said, "But Mommy, you are never home."

"How can I be, as long there are little girls and boys in this world, some no bigger than you, who *have* no home?"

With her mother's life and lap so full of faceless girls and boys, Shelby felt she had been blessed to find a lap in books. That wasn't a bad thing at all. It had given her a love of storytelling, of words, of drama at an early age. As for her parents, even at their busiest, they had always assured her they were only a phone call away. Shelby prepared for bed, then dialed their number. No one was home. She wasn't surprised. Just a little lonely. That too passed as she snuggled up with her pillow and prayed for Jake's losses, and Paula's and Joy's, too, before sharing her hurt and confusion over Patrick with God.

I was so sure he was the one, Lord. The matter was settled in my mind. So settled, that tonight, when Jake touched me, my first response was guilt. Her second was pleasure. That was harder to admit, and even harder to sort out why it was so. Salve for her bruised ego, she decided, and drifted off to sleep.

Chapter Six

The faint fragrance of Shelby's perfume lingered in Jake's office as he sat down to work on business accounts. Shelby had left the computer on screensaver. The darkened screen lit up at his touch, illuminating double-spaced lines of words.

Jake read several paragraphs before he realized it was Shelby's story. He couldn't read this. Shouldn't. Intriguing, though. Words from her mind, making pictures in his:

> Jack straddled a chair. He nudged his glasses to the bridge of his nose and faced Cheryl across the table. "So what's this all about?"
>
> "I've been working for Mr. Weedman, cutting weeds out of fields," said Cheryl.
>
> Jack couldn't corral his grin. "Weed bustin' Weedman. That name for real?"
>
> "Yeah, it's a hoot. Like Cookin' Jack Cook." But Cheryl wasn't laughing. "The joke's on me. I think Mr. Weedman has skipped town."

"Without paying you?"

Cheryl's bottom lip quivered. "If this is justice, it stinks! I worked hard, and I want my money."

Jack hated scenes. Tears made him queasy. Especially in Cheryl's eyes.

"Track them down, Jack," she pleaded. "Be a piece of cake for you."

Cheryl stopped short, her gaze riveted on a spot over Jack's left shoulder.

Jack knew without turning that Tara had slipped into the room. He could smell her exotic perfume.

Three's a crowd. Oldest conflict since Adam, Eve and the snake. Jake reached for the arrow key and wrestled his conscience. Accidental trespass was one thing. But to keep reading took intrusion to another level. Then again, it was written to be read, and she hadn't exactly made it inaccessible.

Conscience gagged and bound, Jake scrolled to the next chapter and found the viewpoint had shifted. The story was now from Tara's point of view:

Tara stretched a slim manicured hand to Cheryl. "I'm Tara Hilton. I'm here visiting from Chicago. And you're...?"

"Cheryl Williams."

"It's nice to meet you, Cheryl." Tara gripped Cheryl's hand, noting callused palms and ragged, broken nails. "I couldn't help overhearing. How can I help?"

"Like I was telling Jack, no one's seen Wiley Weedman or his wife in two days. And believe me, I've walked my feet off looking.''

Tara noted Cheryl's green T-shirt imprinted with the slogan, Weed Busters! We Take Your Field Through a Cleaning. ''So tell me, how long have you known the Weedmans?''

''Do you mind?'' Jack interrupted. His frown melted away as he turned back to Cheryl. ''We can go in the other room, Cheryl, if you'd rather not discuss this in front of a perfect stranger.''

''I'm not all that perfect,'' Tara interjected mildly.

''You think?'' he muttered.

Tara overlooked his sarcasm, and his invitation to butt out and replied, ''So where do we start?''

''*I'll* start by calling some farmers,'' said Jack, emphasis on the singular. ''Get their make on the guy. Whose fields did you weed?''

''Mr. Blatchford's was the last one we did. I've forgotten the other names, but Dudley will know,'' said Cheryl.

''Who's Dudley?'' asked Tara.

''A guy from school,'' said Cheryl. ''He worked for Weedman, too, until he and Weedman quarreled last week. I couldn't hear what it was about, but I could see their faces. Dudley was hot.''

''What else is new?'' said Jack darkly.

Cheryl shrugged and murmured, ''He's been nice to me. He even let me borrow his truck.''

''You told him you were coming to see me, and he gave you his truck keys?''

''I didn't tell him where I was going,'' Cheryl admitted.

"What is it with you and this Dudley guy?" Tara asked Jack.

But Jack was already out of his chair. "I'll make some calls."

"Dudley and Jack compete for checkered flags," Cheryl confided as Jack's footfalls faded into the next room.

"Checkered flags?" echoed Tara.

"They both race beaters out at the Spoon River Speedway. The hobo division," explained Cheryl. "Dudley bumped Jack and spun him out just short of the victory line last summer. It put him out of contention for the championship. Dudley swears it was an accident. But Jack's been down on him ever since."

"So whose side are you on?"

"I'm not taking sides so long as they both treat me right. Shh!" warned Cheryl. "Here comes Jack."

"Can you describe Mr. Weedman?" Tara asked Cheryl as if there had been no detour in the conversation.

"Medium tall. His hair's turning gray. He's kind of old, fifty, maybe sixty. Oh, and he's got scars on his left hand and he's missing the tip of his ring finger."

"That's Weedman you're describing?" Jack jumped into the conversation.

"You've met him?" asked Tara, swinging her foot.

"No. But I've seen him at the post office. Just didn't have a name for the face." Jack fished his keys from his pocket. "I'm going to run by his place and have a look."

"I'll follow in the truck," said Cheryl.

"I may as well come, too. It beats waiting around for Dad," Tara said, uncrossing her legs.

Jack looked pained as she rose from her chair. But he didn't argue when she followed Cheryl out.

Cheryl climbed into a battered old truck and revved the motor. Tara took one look at the springs erupting from the truck seat, smoothed her designer jeans and called to Jack, "On second thought, I'll ride with you."

Tara climbed into Jack's vintage Bel Air. It was immaculate, the seats so slick, it was hard to keep a grip. It made long work of six short blocks. She asked questions along the way, none of which Jack answered to her satisfaction.

Hot shot, thought Tara. Obviously, it didn't occur to him that she might be of help. He parked behind Cheryl and cut the motor.

Tara climbed out. "Whose van?" she called to Cheryl.

"Mr. Weedman's," Cheryl replied. "But no one's here. I've all but beat the door down, trying to get an answer."

Tara gaped at the two-story house. Paint-bare. Shredded window screens. Leaning porch. Unclipped grass.

The gate was wired shut. Jack vaulted the fence and climbed the rotting porch steps. Tara unwired the gate, picked her way up the rickety steps and waited, hopeful someone would answer Jack's knock.

No one did. Jack tried the door.

"You aren't going in are you?" Cheryl called

to them from the grass.

"I would, but it's locked," Jack said. "I'll have a look around back. You two better wait in the car."

Cheryl strode back to the street. But Tara thrust her hand into her pocketbook. Jack's big baby blues widened behind smudged lenses as she withdrew a pick set.

"What're you doing with that?" he asked.

Tara slipped the pick into the lock, and let her fingers do the talking. She felt the faint click of the tumbler. The knob turned. "After you," she said, with an ushering sweep of her hand.

For the first time since her arrival, Jack paid grudging approval. But Cheryl went to pieces.

"You guys!" she screeched from the street. "Don't go in there, you'll get us in trouble!"

Tara locked glances with Jack.

"I don't think she's up for this, maybe we'd better wait," he said finally.

We? The word glided over Tara like lotion on a sunburn. She slid the pick set back into her pocketbook and went after Cheryl. "It's okay, Cheryl. We'll figure out another way."

A sound from the floor above jolted Jake out of Shelby's story. He lifted his gaze to the ceiling. Shelby's room was directly overhead. He heard springs creak. She was turning in for the night, no inkling he was meddling in her business.

Quickly, Jake closed her file and opened his own. But it took him a while to complete his update. His mind kept toying with Shelby's story. It was apparent what she had meant by Joy offering inspiration. But

Joy's job circumstances were just a framework. The story was about Shelby. Shelby from the inside. She inhabited her words, the narrative, her characters.

Jake wished he had read the story from the beginning. Temptation whispered that it wasn't too late. She couldn't see him. Hear him. She was up there, clueless. And still, he could not. Already, he felt guilty for invading her privacy.

Shelby awoke the next morning to a quiet house. She showered in a bathroom devoid of feminine frills, got shampoo in her eye and reached blindly for a towel. The towel bar was empty. But a crumpled hand towel lay on the old-fashioned marble sink surround beside the soap and razor and shaving cream. She dried her hands and face and rubbed her eye.

It was a long stretch from the shower to an oak cabinet and a stack of thick towels. She dried and draped herself in a dark man-size one, and painted her face while her curling iron heated. Lacey underclothes, bought with a honeymoon in mind, twisted the knife a bit. She slipped into a cotton shirt, khaki walking shorts and her trusty sneakers.

The bathroom now resembled the aftermath of a female invasion. She tucked her lotions and potions out of sight in the oak cabinet, curled her hair, swept up a sprinkling of bath powder, and made a mental note to put the curling iron away once it had cooled.

There was a note waiting for her downstairs on the kitchen table. Jake had left his insurance man's phone number in the event the promised loaner car didn't materialize. He had also dashed down his own cell phone number, should she need to get in touch with him.

There was a postscript directing her to waffle batter and orange juice in the refrigerator. His kind gesture found a grateful target. Likewise, last evening. She hadn't set out to air her hurt over Patrick. In fact, she had deliberately avoided doing so with friends of much longer acquaintance.

But Jake, tempered by his own loss, had been sympathetic without smothering her. He hadn't judged. And he hadn't condemned Patrick. His impartiality had relieved her of a gut defensiveness on Patrick's behalf.

Since the breakup, she had waited for anger to kick in and burn away her loyalty to Patrick. As yet, that hadn't happened. Since coming here and in getting to know Jake, she had caught a glimpse of herself and just how large a part of her life her writing had become, how all invasive it was. As if it had a life of its own.

She had assumed Patrick, ambitious himself, understood. But apparently, he had expected a more attentive soul mate. Someone who was as close as skin. *Someone who understood what it meant for two lives to become one,* he had said the night he pulled the rug from beneath her. For the first time, she was able to glimpse the storm clouds Patrick had foreseen on the horizon of their future as man and wife.

Perhaps it was for the best. She was able to think that, and the world did not crash in on her. Feeling stronger for it, Shelby poured juice and stepped outside while the waffle iron was heating. Jake's garden glittered in the dew. His boot tracks wandered up and down the tidy rows. She ambled through the peaceful garden, taking whimsical pleasure in matching her steps to the prints he had left in the soil.

Sunshine and a satisfied appetite was a nice prelude to the productive morning of writing that followed. Wiley Weedman, sparked by Joy's account of her missing boss, shaped up nicely as a shady character. Shelby took the liberty of borrowing from Jake's account of Dan Flat's alleged chicanery. When coupled with Mrs. Wiseman's genealogical research, it provided plot answers for who did what and why and foreshadowed the unnatural nature of Wiley Weedman's disappearance.

It was a few minutes after twelve when Joy came with a lunch invitation. Shelby went downstairs and helped Paula put the meal together while Joy set the table.

"Still no sign of Mr. Wiseman?" she asked over a tuna salad sandwich and chips.

"I've given up on fieldwork," Joy said. "I'm helping Mom now."

"In the sign shop?" asked Shelby.

"Jake's strong on keeping the business in the family," Paula explained. "I think she's a little young for bookkeeping. But he urged me to give her some pointers and see if she has the knack."

"Adding, subtracting and writing a few checks. What's the big deal? Say! Maybe he fell in the cistern," Joy suggested, changing the subject.

"Who?"

"Mr. Wiseman," Joy said. "There are two in his backyard."

"Where you had no business," countered Paula.

"He could be dead, Mom."

"Oh, don't be silly!" Paula scolded.

Joy slanted Shelby a look from half-lidded eyes.

Her mouth curled into a faint smirk, as puzzling to Shelby as the purple slivers in the tuna salad.

"Purple basil," Paula told her, solving one mystery.

"From Uncle Jake's garden." Joy dampened her finger and drew a path through the potato chip crumbs on her plate. "Do you know that nightshade is fatal?"

"What's nightshade?" asked Shelby.

"A weed. When I was working cutting weeds out of beans, Uncle Jake warned me not to throw any nightshade over fences where livestock might eat it. Suppose it's fatal to people, too?" she asked, and sucked the salt off her fingers.

"Where are your manners?" complained Paula. "Stop licking your fingers."

"Sorry. How do you plot a mystery?" Joy asked Shelby.

"By asking 'what if?'" Shelby answered. "What if he isn't what he appears to be? What if she learns his secret? What if he discovers she knows? What if—"

"Mr. Wiseman is dead of nightshade?" Joy interjected.

"Joy, would you please give it a rest?" Paula said. "Rinse your plate if you're finished."

Joy dumped her dishes into the sink. "I'm out of here."

"Don't leave the yard," Paula warned.

Joy made a face and ambled out with her can of soda.

"She's grounded and I'm suffering. Go figure." Paula pushed her lunch aside and rose with a sigh to put the remaining dishes in the dishwasher.

"Leave those, I'll get them," said Shelby.

When Paula had gone, Shelby filled the sink with hot soapy water. As she washed dishes, she ironed the wrinkles out of the next story scene. Back in Jake's office, the words formed in her mind and trickled from her fingers to the keys like hot fudge over ice cream. By midafternoon, her teen sleuths had stumbled upon the late Mr. Weedman. The scene was a little rough.

Shelby let it breathe and polished what she had written that morning. She worked uninterrupted until Jake and Gram Kate came home. And still the grasping tentacles of her story held her in place. She was giving her revisions a hasty read when Jake knocked on the open door.

"Are you still working?"

"Just finished." Shelby closed her file. "I was thinking—it's about my turn to fix dinner. What do you like?"

"The sounds of that," he said.

Shelby noticed grease smudges on his shirt and trousers and four o'clock shadow darkening his jaw. His hair was tousled with a line of demarcation in chestnut waves where his cap usually rested. She smiled. "Did you have a rough day?"

"A long ride, mostly. We did a job up by Joliet." He leaned a shoulder against the doorjamb and hooked his fingertips in his pocket, adding, "I picked up Gram on the way home. She's in the kitchen, washing tomatoes. How are you with bacon-and-tomato sandwiches?"

"One of my favorites," said Shelby.

"Good. I'll grab a quick shower and come help you keep Gram out of the matches."

They traded smiles. He turned away and back again to ask, "How's the car?"

"The car!" Shelby pressed the heel of her hand to her forehead. "It slipped my mind."

"No one knocked or rang the bell?" asked Jake.

"If they did, I didn't hear them." Shelby crossed to the window and looked out at the white midsize sedan parked beside his Jeep. "Not that that means anything. I warned you, when I write…"

"Comatose, I know." He grinned.

"I'll take it for a spin after supper," Shelby said. "Would you like to come along?"

"Sure. It's black raspberry season. I know a good patch," Jake replied. "A berry pie sounds good, don't you think?"

"Second only to butter bean cake."

Laughter lit Jake's eyes. The ringing phone spared Shelby from admitting that she wasn't a pie baker. She went downstairs to help Gram Kate with dinner preparations.

Over dinner, Jake regaled them with a tale of rescuing a kitten from a tree using his bucket truck.

His story sparked a memory in Shelby. "I called the fire department once to rescue my kittens from the pool house roof." She smiled, remembering. "An ordinary ladder would have done it. But my mother was hostessing a fund-raiser, the housekeeper didn't speak English and I was unwilling to wait. Mom got pretty upset when the fire truck came through the gates. Everyone crowded out into the backyard to see what was burning."

Jake laughed. "You must have been a lively tyke."

"My goodness, yes, she was live…live…oh,"

murmured Gram. She nudged the platter of bacon Jake's way.

"No seconds for me, Gram. I'm saving room for pie."

Gram cocked her head to one side. "Did I make pie?"

"No, Gram. But Shelby and I are going to, once we get the berries picked. You do bake, don't you Shelby?" he asked.

"Only at the beach." Shelby rubbed her cheeks as if coating them in suntan oil.

Jake laughed, secretly appreciative of that fine white skin. "Scratch the pie, we'll go the beach," he said and rose to answer the ringing phone.

Chapter Seven

It was Paula on the phone. The man who dropped the loaner car by had left the keys with her. She had slipped the keys into her pocket, and forgot them until she arrived home.

"We were just talking about taking a drive after dinner," Jake told her. "Ask Joy if she'd mind keeping Gram company for an hour or so. Or is she not allowed out?"

"Hey! I'm a reasonable woman, I'll send her over as soon as we've eaten," Paula said cheerfully.

Joy showed up a short while later with crochet thread for Gram Kate, keys for Shelby and a kiss for her uncle Jake.

"Thanks for cutting me loose, I was going stir crazy," she muttered and rolled her eyes.

"Must be contagious, your mom has a touch of it, too," Jake said.

"You don't care if I use your computer, do you, Uncle Jake?" Joy asked, breezing on through the kitchen. "Gram? Are you coming? Don't forget your crocheting."

At Jake's suggestion, Shelby changed clothes for their berry-picking expedition. She came downstairs dressed in a pair of slim-fitting white slacks and a pink-and-white knit T-shirt that gently shaped itself to her contours. Jake pushed away from the porch pillar, enjoying the perfect foil her delicate skin made for the deep-pink trim that edged the scooped neck and cap sleeves of her shirt.

"Do these berries grow anywhere near a soybean field?" Shelby asked as they crossed the yard to the car.

"Hadn't thought about it. Why?"

"Call it research. Would you mind?"

"Not at all," Jake replied. He held the car door for her as she slid behind the wheel, and circled to the passenger's side.

The evening sun flowed through the windshield, warming Shelby's skin as they left the town behind and set out for Wildwood. A rabbit darted across the road a few miles farther along as she slowed for the lane.

"Is the berry patch reserved for Wildwood guests?" she asked, glancing away from the road to watch the rabbit dart safely into roadside grasses.

"The patch isn't here, we're taking the long way so I can show you a soybean field," Jake explained.

"Berries, soybeans. I'm beginning to see that there's a good deal more to Wildwood than meets the eye," Shelby said.

"It's a combination working farm and vacation site," replied Jake. He reached across the seat, honked the horn and waved to a young man sprawled beneath a tractor.

"That's Rick. He didn't know beans about tinkering when he started coming out here a few years ago. Trace took him under his wing, now there's not a piece of machinery on the place he can't fix. Pull over and we'll ask him about walking through the beans."

Jake rolled down his window, and made introductions. A dark-eyed handsome young man, Rick asked Shelby if she cared to take a hoe along.

"For the weeds?" she countered.

"No, the snakes," he replied.

Shelby shot Jake an alarmed glance.

"He's pulling your leg." Jake chuckled.

Rick conceded it with a grin, waved them on and went back to his tractor repairs.

The ruts Shelby followed per Jake's directions skirted pasture and a cornfield. The dirt trail ended at a body of trees and a creek. Drawn by the tranquil babbling of a tree-lined creek, she climbed out and found her way to the water's edge. Jake retrieved two plastic pails from the back seat of the car. He caught up with her at the creek where she perched on the bank, dangling a stick into the water, knees bent, her feet tucked beneath her.

Peering up at him, she asked, "How deep is the water?"

"Two, maybe three feet," Jake said, seeing her eyes water in the same leaf-dappled sunlight that caught fire in her hair. "There's a footbridge upstream."

Shelby took the berry pail and the hand up Jake offered, but dropped it again once she was on her feet. A campground came into view as they strolled side by side toward a bend in the creek.

"Sounds like the kids are singing for their supper." Jake pointed out a steel building set back in the trees on the other side of the creek.

Shelby stopped to listen to young voices mingling with bird cries and humming insects. A summer camp veteran, the familiar song wafting on the evening air brought back poignant memories of bouts with homesickness. "Church camp?"

Jake nodded. "Kids camps, retreats, family camps, Wildwood has it all."

"And the...cottages?" she faltered, leaving out *honeymoon.*

"Farther along, there in the pines," Jake said, wondering at her thoughts.

Shelby determined not to look should they pass within view of the cottages. Rejection and the memories it tarnished was tough enough without a visual aid of the honeymoon cabin.

The path narrowed, crowded by trees and undergrowth. Shelby fell behind Jake as they crossed the creek on a narrow bridge that brought them to the edge of the pines. So guarded was she against a chance glimpse of the threshold she had not crossed, she dropped her gaze to the path, and in so doing bumped into Jake when he stopped.

"Oops. Sorry," she began, when he turned with a warning finger to his lip, and pointed down the path. The vista opened to a rolling field. Alongside the field grazed two deer.

Shelby watched, transfixed, as the young buck's head came up. The doe lifted her head, too, then bounded after the buck across a pasture and into the woods.

"Beautiful!" Shelby exclaimed, thrilled at the sight.

Jake thought the same of her shining eyes and flushed cheeks. He held back a sapling so as not to let it snap back on her as they resumed walking. "Trace complains they get more than their share of the corn crop. But he wouldn't trade them for money in the bank."

Shelby returned his smile and lengthened her step to walk beside him as they left the woods behind. Planted rows stretched straight and neat and flowed together on the distant horizon. She stooped at the edge of the field and rested on the balls of her feet to pick up a handful of rich black dirt. Murmuring at the moistness of it, she let it sift through her fingers, then scooped again and breathed of its earthy fragrance.

The childlike exploration of ordinary dirt from one wrapped in so womanly a frame quickened Jake's pulse. He shifted his feet. She lifted her face and caught him watching her.

"That your research?" he quipped.

Color rose to her cheeks, heightening her appeal. "Just seeing what it smells like."

"What's the verdict?"

Her mouth tipped at his gentle teasing. "Pretty much the same as city dirt, I guess," she said, and dusted her hands.

There was dirt on the tip of her nose and a curve to her mouth that just begged to be kissed. Jake hunkered down beside her, but on closer examination deemed the impulse reckless. He checked it and plucked a soybean frond from an ankle-high plant. "You left a little research on your nose." He dusted her nose with the bean plant, then grinned and tickled her cheek with it.

The leaf was green velvet against Shelby's skin. His gesture was playful, but distracting just by virtue of her awareness of his fingertips touching her skin. "Soybean?" she asked.

He nodded.

"Soft," she said.

So was her cheek, and the fingers that brushed his as the snippet changed hands. Shelby averted her gaze and in less time than it took to fold the soybean frond into her pocket, was on her feet.

"Ready to go?" Jake asked. He cupped a hand to her elbow and nudged her to the center soil between two rows. It was too narrow for walking side by side. His hand fell away. He stepped over a row of beans and led the way across the field where the fading sun basked a second grove of trees in silvery green light. The berry bushes he had mentioned grew at the edge of the woods.

"This is state property," Jake said. "Keep walking, and you'll run into a dump."

Shelby wrinkled her nose. "Is that what I smell?"

"It's not that kind of dump. It's broken-up road beds and a graveyard of old equipment," said Jake. "There are some grain bins, too. It could be wet corn we smell. Or a dead animal. We'll go the other way. Maybe we can get upwind of it."

They soon came upon a second flush of wild black raspberry bushes. The brambles climbed a steep embankment. Jake left the easy picking to Shelby, and scaled to the top for the less accessible berries.

"Plip, plip, plip, I don't hear yours plipping," she called.

"The bottom of the pail is covered," he said, playing along. "Berries are floating in, not making a sound."

"That, or you're sleeping on the job," she countered. "Ouch! I'm caught on the bush. I should have worn long sleeves. You didn't mention the bushes were full of stickers."

"If you pick as good as you complain, we'll have enough for a pie in no time."

"I've picked them clean, I do believe. See here?"

Jake scanned the bushes and stretched his free hand down to her. "Those are beginner's bushes. Take off the training wheels and hack your way up here with the master berry pickers," he challenged.

"Is there enough to keep both of us picking?" she asked.

"And then some," he claimed.

Berry canes snagged Shelby's T-shirt, slowing progress. She hooked the handle of her pail over her arm and gripped Jake's hand with both of hers. But the bank was steep and slick from recent rain. She lost her footing and toppled into the ditch, squealing.

Jake spilled his bucket of berries, trying to reach her. "Are you okay?"

"Except for my pride and your berries." Flushed and giggling, she tried to get her feet. "I'm stuck! Where's a crane when you need one?"

Jake laughed and gripped her berry-stained hands. He hauled her to her feet, and up the bank before letting go. "You'll have to pick fast to redeem yourself."

"I will, will I?" she countered.

"That's right. A pail of berries before it gets dark."

"Is that enough for a pie?"

"More than," said. "You want make a race of it?"

"What're the stakes?"

"The loser bakes the pie. Deal?"

Reasoning the advantage was hers now that he had spilled his berries, she grinned and cried, "On your mark, set, go!"

Fingers flying, Shelby plucked the sweet ripe berries by the handful. But her pail was only half full when shadows draped the nearby woodlands in shades as deep as the berries.

"Better go," Jake said

"Don't tell me you've filled your pail already!"

"No. But if we don't start back now, we'll be stumbling along in the dark."

Shelby checked the contents of his pail, comparing it to hers. "Close," she said.

Jake grinned and helped her down the embankment. The setting sun was behind them as they crossed the field. When they reached the creek and looked back, it had slipped below the horizon. It sent up rays, gold-leafing the edges of pink-and-lavender clouds.

"Gorgeous," Shelby said, stopping beside Jake to admire the sky. "I love a pretty sunset."

"They're all pretty."

"Even the gray ones?" she asked.

At her smile, he couldn't remember gray. "All of them."

"I needed this," she conceded, as they resumed walking.

"We've had nice rains. Makes the berries plump and sweet," he said, and plopped a handful into his mouth.

"Not the berries. This," she said and stretched her free arm as if to embrace creation itself. "Days get so rushed, it's easy to neglect the simple things."

Understanding came with a smile. Shelby smiled, too. It moved over Jake like a tender glance, that quiet brush of souls that words would only diminish.

They had dawdled long enough that darkness fell en route to the car. "Watch out for the stump there." Familiar with the terrain, Jake made the most of it and caught Shelby's hand under the guise of guiding her safely along.

Her fingers were sticky with berry juice. His were, too. A working hand, strong and scuffed and callused. Solid, like the man. Shelby thought of retrieving her hand, but didn't. Choosing not to examine her reasons too closely she hummed beneath her breath as they ambled the path back to the car. On the ride home, she fell silent, content to watch the thumbnail moon ascend and shoulder the stars about.

"How about a tiebreaker?" asked Jake as he slowed for the road into town.

"A pie-breaker?"

He chuckled. "You heard me the first time."

"I write better than I bake," Shelby said mildly.

"I'll introduce you to Gram's fail-proof recipe."

"Not so fast," she protested. "I may not need a recipe. There is a good chance I won this contest."

"Prove it," he countered.

"We'll count them," Shelby said, reaching for her pail.

"Inconclusive. I ate some of mine," claimed Jake.

"Too bad," she said.

Jake laughed. He hit the dimmer switch on the headlights and sang, "She can bake a cherry pie fast as a cat can wink its eye. But she's a young thing and cannot leave her mother."

"Watch it, charming Billy. Pedestrians," Shelby warned, and poured his berries into her pail while he was busy giving his side of the road to two joggers.

Jake stretched an arm along the back of the seat, cuffed her shoulder, and resumed singing, "She can bake a berry pie, fast as a cat can wink its eye. But she's a berry thief and berry thieves barely ever win."

Jake checked on Gram as soon as they arrived home. She had retired for the night. He turned out the light she had left on, and joined Shelby at the kitchen sink.

She looked up from washing the berries. "You mentioned a recipe."

"In here." Jake reached into the cupboard over her head for a cedar box recipe file. "I'll run Joy home and be right back to help," he promised and left her flipping through file cards.

Joy was in Jake's office, glued to the computer screen. She gave a start when he bumped the desk.

"Pry yourself away, and I'll—" Seeing guilt leap to her face, Jake glanced from her face to the screen and back again. "What're you up to now?"

"Nothing," she said and fumbled for the mouse.

Jake caught her wrist before she could clear the screen. "Let's have a look."

"It isn't anything, honest."

"Scoot." Jake waved her out of his chair and away from the keyboard. He scanned a few lines, then bolted out of the chair, scolding, "Joy! You shouldn't be reading this. It's Shelby's story."

"Is it?" Joy paused in the midst of feigned innocence, and narrowed her eyes. "Say, how do *you* know what it is?"

Heat swept up Jake's neck. "Get your stuff together. Your mom will be calling," he replied, dodging her shrewd question.

"She already did," replied Joy. "Twice. I thought you were picking berries."

"We were."

"After dark?"

"Don't change the subject," growled Jake. "That's twice now you've poked your nose into her business."

"Have a cat, why don't you?" Joy flounced out of her chair, pushed out her bottom lip and didn't say a word until Jake stopped the Jeep in front of her house.

"Don't tell on me and I won't tell on you," she said, changing tactics.

Irritated, Jake countered, "Get out before I turn you over my knee."

"We have a deal, then?" she said, so close to gloating, Jake reached as if to make good on his threat.

Joy scrambled out of the Jeep, backed off a yard and drew a finger across her lips. "Mum's the word, partner."

Trapped by his own duplicity, Jake clamped his jaw tight.

Joy flung her backpack over her shoulder and tramped inside. It wasn't good for her, getting away with it. Jake knew that. But he didn't care much for the alternative.

Shelby was in the kitchen, up to her elbows in flour when Jake arrived home. Hearing him come in, she ceased humming "Billy Boy," swung around and flung her arms wide, trying to screen her pie makings on the counter behind her. "Stop! You can't see until it's in the oven."

"Will that be anytime soon?" He glossed over a guilty conscience with friendly banter.

She cast the clock a frowning glance. "At present rate, we'll be having pie for breakfast."

"I'll make the filling," he offered. "You finish the crust, and we'll have hot pie à la mode out in the hammock under the stars."

"I'm having a little trouble," she admitted.

Jake peered through the arch between her out-stretched arm and her side. A lumpy wad of dough was caught on the counter between two pieces of waxed paper. He shifted his gaze to her face. She had been eating berries. The evidence at the corner of her mouth distracted him. "Try a little more flour," he said.

"You try. Okay?"

Jake washed his hands, motioned her aside, and peeled away the waxed paper.

Shelby's doleful gaze skipped from her lump of dough to his tactfully held mouth. "Hopeless?" she asked.

"Not at all. It's a fair start."

"That's what I thought," she said, and wrinkled her nose. "Can you fix it?"

Jake divided the dough and returned half to the

bowl. He moistened the counter so the waxed paper wouldn't slip.

"It didn't mention that on the recipe," said Shelby.

"It's a tip from Gram Kate." Jake stepped back and offered her the rolling pin. "Your turn. Get a nice firm grip on the handles. Go on, take it."

Shelby took his place at the counter. The light gleamed on her white neck and red-gold tresses. Jake stepped closer, drawn by curls on cream and her light, sweet scent. She gave the pie dough a nudge with the pin.

"Put some pressure to it," he urged. "That's the way."

"Are you sure you wouldn't like to do this yourself?"

"You'll get the hang of it." Jake stepped behind her and covered her hands on the rolling pin. "Try it like this."

Shelby drew a breath and held it. Jake could feel it, trapped there between them, as surely as the small white hands trapped beneath his. The skin-to-skin sensation transmitted itself to him like static traveling nerve endings.

"Keep it light, but firm, that's it," he murmured, his voice growing thick as the filling yet to be made. "Now the other way. Make each pass count. Reach out there now and give the paper a turn," he said and moved his hand.

She turned the waxed paper with its half-formed pie crust, then turned herself, too. Caught between him and the counter, she lowered her lashes, unable to meet what she had kindled in his eyes. "I've got it now."

Her subdued manner, the scent of her perfume, and thick-lashed eyes that wouldn't hold Jake's gaze filled his senses. He brushed flour from her cheek with a touch that turned into a caress. But she caught his wrist.

"Don't, Jake," she murmured, before he could cover her berry-stained mouth in kisses.

"You sure?" His voice fell to a corn husk whisper.

"It isn't... It's just that..."

"I'm not pressing you," he said. "I like what I see, that's all."

"But when you say that..." she began.

"You're over thinking this."

"I need some time," she said, heart beating hard.

Jake turned the hand that held his wrist. Matched his palm to hers. Moist and firm, like her mouth telling him no. Easy to look at, hard to hear. He shifted his weight, giving her space. Let go of her hand and the other one, too, and sought words with the right inflection so as to bridge the moment: "Two tablespoons of flour, a pat of butter and sugar to taste. There's a saucepan on the stove. You don't want to cook it, just thicken the berries."

"Jake?"

He looked to find her chewing her lip, anxiety tugging at her eyes and mouth.

"Never mind. I'll make it," he said, letting her off the hook.

"We can still be friends, can't we?" said Shelby.

"I was talking about the pie. I'll make the pie."

Color swept up her ivory neck, staining her cheeks. Her lashes fell, making dusky shadows beneath her eyes. Remorse washed over him. Her words were innocent and well-intentioned. His were duck and cover. Even now, pride had him by the throat. He turned away and ran his finger down the recipe card to keep from saying anything else to be sorry for later.

"I'm not much help here, am I?" she said into the clock-ticking tap-dripping silence. "I think I'll call it a night. If you don't mind finishing it by yourself."

"Sure. Go on," he replied.

"Leave the dishes. I'll clean the kitchen tomorrow," she said before slipping up the stairs and leaving him all by his lonesome.

Chapter Eight

Shelby kicked herself all the way up the stairs. It shouldn't have taken a caress to make her aware of the feelings awakening in Jake. But a relationship gone south and her preoccupation with getting on with life had blinded her to the subtleties of...

Oh, who was she kidding? What subtleties? Jake didn't have to spell it out in neon. His frankness on the heels of that almost-kiss was no more than what she should have anticipated. He'd been silently appraising her with those sky-blue eyes of his almost from the moment they met. His appreciative glances drove back shadows and her battered ego responded in gratitude. And why not? He was an enterprising, good-natured, rugged man's man, his even-keeled personality seasoned with humor and a tenderness for God and family.

Her heart was still rocking; she had come so close to walking into his arms. But it was the rejected part that missed being held and kissed and regarded as unique and worth waiting for. *Wasn't it?* Her hidden self cringed, shrinking from razor sharp reflection. Yet if she couldn't be honest, what was left to distinguish between writing fiction and living it?

Was it time to go home? Before she threw caution to the wind and herself into Jake's arms. Was she that emotionally ragged? She flushed at the thought and tried to wash it away in the shower. At length, she crawled into bed, then out again and to her knees, seeking a sign from God as to what feelings to trust, what to dismiss as tremors and aftershocks, and what to do about Jake.

Jake made short work of the pie and sugared the top crust. But his interest in pie making had fled up the stairs. The arms she had held up to screen her pie from him also held him at bay. Her heart was still living in the past, and his had turned with tenderness for her. If she lived down the street or in the next town, he would bide his time. But she would leave in a few days, and he would know her no better than he knew her right now. *Except through her written words.*

Jake cleaned up the kitchen and made a pot of coffee. He took a cup with him to his study, tucked his conscience into bed, and opened Shelby's file. Starting at the beginning, he took his time, relishing the bits and pieces of Shelby dispersed throughout her characters. His coffee had cooled by the time he reached the additions she had made since last night's reading:

Tara heard a garbage can rattle.

"What was that?" cried Cheryl.

Tara pivoted to see Jack ease around the side

of Weedman's house and out of sight.

"You guys! You're trespassing all over the place!" Cheryl's hoarse whisper trailed after Tara.

"Shh!" Tara pressed into sun-soaked siding. Inched around the house. Made the far corner as a shout rang out. She scanned the backyard, heart in her throat. Tangled grass. Weeds. All of it moving as if by a maverick breeze.

Tara tripped over a bulky tarp. She fell as the canvas moved beneath her. She had fallen on top of Jack!

"My glasses!" Jack's muffled cry brought her scrambling to her feet.

At the same moment, a figure sprang from the moving grass and bolted for the barberry hedge bordering the back alley.

Tara lunged after the fleeing figure and caught a handful of T-shirt. But he outmuscled her and jerked free. She weighed her concern for Jack against the odds of catching his assailant, factored in barbed branches and pricey jeans. She turned back.

"Jack? Are you okay?" Tara cried.

Jack crawled from beneath the crumpled tarp and flung a blind glance toward the hedge. "Where'd he go? Did he get away?"

"I couldn't hold him." Tara eagle-eyed his glasses, scooped them up unbroken and dropped them into his hand. "Who was it?"

"I don't know. Tarp hit me out of nowhere. Had a body behind it. Hit the ground hard. Must have knocked the wind out of me." Jake put on his glasses and staggered to his feet.

"Did you get a look?"

"Male. Five-eleven. Muscular—160 or 170 pounds. Green T-shirt, jeans, a baseball cap." Tara rattled off his assailant's description.

"Dudley," growled Jake. "Figures."

"Where do we find him?" Tara asked, primed to rocket into hot pursuit.

"Ask Cheryl, they're so chummy," Jack growled.

Tara twitched, watching him rein in his emotions. It was a mute and instantaneous exercise interrupted by the hoarse roar of a motor coming to life. "The truck!" she cried.

Jake sped past Tara. She circled the house at his heels as Dudley tore away, his truck tires spitting rocks and burning rubber. Cheryl stood in the avenue, shielding her face and shouting after him.

Jake reread the last few paragraphs again. Three times, Shelby had typed *Jake* instead of Jack. He was intrigued by the mistake, and by the dangled carrot of a love triangle in which hearts were sure to be skinned.

The buttery sweet fragrance of fruit and baking pastry wafted throughout the house. All that remained to be read was bare-boned plot with snatches of dialogue. Stray thoughts and incomplete sentences trailed off into wide gaps between paragraphs yet to be filled in. Jake shut down the computer, returned to the kitchen and took the pie from the oven. But his appetite for sweets had been displaced by a yearning that pie could not remedy. He left it to cool uncut, and went to bed.

* * *

Shelby slept poorly. Singing birds ushered in the dawn. Feeling draggy, she pulled a pillow over her head. But sound carried through the feather pillow, footsteps that caught her ear and made her listen. Certain it was Jake going downstairs, she struggled with the proper way to go about leaving. Should she say goodbye in person? Or leave him a note?

The easy out was cold by any standard, and poor return upon the hospitality she had received. Gambling that Jake would take his time over breakfast, she swung out of bed, grabbed her robe and padded into the bathroom.

The blended scents of soap, shaving cream and a tangy aftershave lotion lingered there. Shelby showered quickly in that haze of masculine scent, and donned a sleeveless dress of pale apricot. The bodice was fitted, the skirt free-flowing and comfortable for travel. She dashed a comb through her curls, tinted her lips, and was on her knees, reaching under the bed for her platform sandals, when Jake's Jeep growled to life in the driveway below. Shelby flung open the window and called to him, but couldn't make herself heard over the Jeep. Abandoning her shoe search, Shelby flew barefoot down the steps, through the house and over the dewy grass.

"Jake!" She waved both arms as he backed into the alley.

Jake glanced around, and hit the brakes. His heart leapt to all sorts of conclusions at the sight of her coming after him. He rolled down the window. "You're up early."

"Yes, I know. Good morn— Ouch! Murder!" she muttered, even as his amiable demeanor quieted her fears over last night's honest exchange.

Jake's mouth twitched at the sight of her mincing across white rock, arms spread, fingers cocked. He opened the driver's door. "Climb in, tenderfoot."

"No thanks, I don't want to keep you," Shelby said, breath coming light and shallow and driven by a heavy pulse. "I just wanted to say—"

"I'm in no hurry. Hop in." Jake slid to one side and patted the remaining portion of bucket seat.

Taking pity on her bare feet, Shelby gripped the steering wheel and swung up beside him. The close fit brought him into sharp focus. The shaving nick on his chin. The associated scents. The strength and tautness of his thigh.

"Careful, you'll fall out on your nose." He draped his left arm over her shoulder, stabilizing her precarious perch.

Hastily prepared speech forgotten, Shelby asked, "How'd the pie turn out?"

"Work of art," he said. "You didn't notice? I'm hurt."

His chuckle resounded at close quarters, evoking an answering smile. "I'll admire it in a minute, I promise." She dropped her gaze, tracing with her eye a raveling thread that hung from the hem of his short-sleeved work shirt and curled against hard biceps. "I didn't want to leave without saying goodbye. And telling you how much I appreciate your hospitality."

His smile died. "You're leaving?"

"It's been three days."

"I thought you had a week."

"I do. But I have a car now. I've imposed long enough." Feeling the ease go out of him, Shelby's heart crowded against her ribs. She lifted her lashes to find his eyes gone somber upon his deeply tanned features. *Like lamps keeping watch over sun-glazed prairie.* The description wrote itself upon the tablet of her heart. Swiftly, she averted her gaze to his forefinger, tracing a dusty crack in the steering wheel.

Madness. She condemned the sudden ache to lock his finger with her own. A trapped fly sounded like a chain saw buzzing against the window glass. She bridged the painful silence. "I need to get my computer fixed and tie up some loose ends before I return to work. I have those manuscripts to read yet. And there's my writing, of course."

"If this is about last night…" he began at length.

"It isn't." Shelby gripped the steering wheel, an anchor as he withdrew his arm. Madness paraded, this time as an impulse to turn her face into that hard arm and hold on tight. Instead, she opened the door and let herself down on the bruising white rock.

"You taking off right away?" he asked.

"Noon or so. It's a three-hour drive."

He nodded. "We do jobs up that way occasionally."

"You do?" Shelby replied. "Then perhaps you'd let me take you out to dinner the next time you're in town."

"I might, if you twisted my arm," he said.

She knew it was an illusion. Yet there it was, that sensation of all else falling away, leaving them showered by blue halo. Twin brackets framed and lifted his mouth as he leaned and offered an arm to twist. She smiled and reached past it for the pen in his pocket.

"Paper?"

He gave her a credit card receipt from the dashboard, and when she had jotted down her phone number, traded it for his business card.

"If you ever need a good sign man, give me a call."

"I will," she murmured.

His grin relieved the heaviness over saying goodbye. She had to pack and change the sheets and e-mail her story to herself. But all she wanted to do was look into those eyes looking back at her. Their fingers brushed as she returned his pen, sending a pleasant sensation pulsating up her arm.

"I'll call and let you know next time I have a job in the city. Until then—" he tucked his pen into his pocket, reached for her fingers and gave them a squeeze "—take care of yourself."

"You too. I love…I loved being here," she amended. "In spite of everything."

"You're welcome anytime."

"That's sweet of you. Thank you."

He pressed her hand once more, and let it go.

She watched him drive away, and hugged herself. *Love him?* She hardly knew him. Her slipping tongue was the sign she sought, the billboard spelling out in urgent letters, Go Home!

Shelby trekked back through the kitchen, and saw that Jake had tidied it. The coffee in the coffeepot on the counter was still hot. She poured herself a cup, and noticed the pie. It was uncut on the counter. Picture perfect. But pies weren't made to be admired for their beauty.

The pie smirked in its wholeness charging her with crimes against the pie baker. She had disappointed him. Stolen his joy. Deprived him of company after all the trouble of prickly bushes and spilled berries and time spent making and baking.

Shelby threatened the pie with knife, plate and server. It sneered, daring her to help herself. But how could she when Jake had not? She was covering her crimped and crusted accuser in plastic wrap when Jake's sister Christine came for Gram Kate. Gram Kate urged them to have some pie. The dear soul thought she had baked it herself. Shelby declined. But Gram talked Christine into having a piece. She cut a slice for herself, too, then replaced the wrap over the remaining pie and gave it to Christine to take home and share with her family.

Shelby felt badly that Jake's sweet tooth was in for a disappointment. Unable to help, she tried to dismiss it, and padded into his office to e-mail her story home. With time to spare, she reworked yesterday's rough draft. As always, time fell away as the story pulled her in:

"What was he doing here, anyway?" Tara asked as Dudley streaked away, his pickup truck oil-burning a trail of smoke.

"Helping look for Mr. Weedman, I suppose," said Cheryl.

"Some help," muttered Jack.

As Jack popped his knuckles and brooded, Tara explained how Dudley had knocked Jack to the ground and flung the tarp over him.

"I'm sure he didn't mean to hurt you, he probably just wanted to get away unseen," Cheryl said.

"You think?" Jack said.

Cheryl sniffed. Tara looked from one to the

other, but didn't venture a comment.

Jack fished his keys out of his pocket. "No use hanging around here. Come on, let's get going."

Tara slid into the front seat after Cheryl, and closed the passenger's door. "Where to?"

"Blatchford Farms," Jack replied.

"Blatchford? The farm is named for the town?" Tara asked.

"No. The town is named after Mr. Blatchford's great-granddaddy."

"Drop me off at home, would you Jack?" Cheryl spoke up as Jack pulled away from the curb.

"You're not coming with us?" Jack asked.

"Mom's expecting me home to watch the kids. Let me know what you find out."

Jack slowed for a mobile home park at the edge of town. Tara climbed out to let Cheryl out of the car.

"Catch you later," Cheryl said.

A short drive in the country took Jack and Tara past thriving green fields and up a gravel lane. Jack stopped in front of a handsome house with deep porches and tall white columns.

"Nice place," Tara commented, admiring the commanding view of countryside.

"It's on the register of historic homes. Mr. Blatchford's proud of his heritage," Jack told her. "You coming?"

"Wouldn't miss it," Tara said, swinging her door wide.

Jack led the way to the porch where geraniums blossomed in hanging pots, and fans rotated lazily overhead. A little black dog darted out between the feet of the woman who answered the bell.

"Sugar!" cried the housekeeper, hands in her hair. "Catch her before she strikes a rabbit trail and runs off again."

Jack leapt after the dog. "Here Sugar, here Sugar!"

His tone clashed with the sweetness of the name. Tara giggled and trailed them across the yard, singing.

The dog darted straight for the field with no sign of slowing. Jack tore after him, leaping over rows of shin-high beans. Tara's lightheartedness gave way to alarm at the speed with which the dog was outdistancing Jack. "Stop chasing her, you're scaring her," she warned.

Jake stopped. But only because his trailing shoestring tripped him. He sprawled headlong in the dirt. Sugar slowed to a trot, then stopped a short distance away and began digging. Whining. Yelping, front paws showering dirt.

Tara stood by, trying to catch her breath as Jake tied his shoe.

"Okay, I'll go this way and you go thataway," he whispered on the way to his feet.

Tara noticed a rank odor as she crept forward, and wrinkled her nose. "Phew. What is that?"

"I don't know, don't worry about it. Inch up there and grab her."

Tara reached for Sugar's collar, then froze and gaped with unbelieving eyes. Jutting out of the dirt between the dog's paws was a human hand. Scarred. With a missing finger. She shrieked in horror.

Jack bounded to her side, and recoiled, too. All the color drained from his face. "Good gravy, you've found Weedman!"

"How do you..." All at once, Cheryl's remembered description split Tara's drumming ears. The missing finger. She covered her face and didn't look again.

Shelby heard voices in the kitchen and saw that it was noon. Quickly, she reread her story, corrected typos, turning several *Jakes* into *Jacks,* and e-mailed her story to her home computer.

Paula sent Joy with a lunch invitation. With Joy's help, Shelby secured the file so that it was safe to leave on Jake's computer until she arrived home and made a backup.

"Then I'll call you and you can delete it for me, okay?" said Shelby.

"Sure, no problem," Joy agreed. "Guess what? Mrs. Wiseman's car is home. Dirk called and told me."

Chagrined at the realization her story character, Mr. Weedman, was more real to her than Joy's boss, Mr. Wiseman, Shelby said, "I suppose that solves that mystery, then."

"If he's with her, it will."

"You don't know?" asked Shelby.

"Not yet," Joy answered. "When I talked to Dirk, he said none of the crew showed up this morning, so he went home, too. Does Uncle Jake know you're leaving?" She turned from the matter at hand.

"Yes."

"What'd he say? Was he upset?" Joy asked.

"Hardly. What makes you ask?" Shelby returned.

"Aunt Wendy said...oh, never mind," Joy replied. "She's kind of silly sometimes."

Mapped amidst the curiosity of Joy's expression was relief. Shelby didn't quite know what to make of it, so she dismissed it, and thanked Joy for all her help. "If you ever get to Chicago, give me a call and we'll get together."

"Sure, whatever," Joy agreed offhandedly.

Paula was disappointed to learn Shelby was leaving. She had brought a casserole for lunch. Finding it hard to turn her down, Shelby accepted her lunch invitation graciously, and helped make a salad while Paula reheated the casserole in the microwave.

When they had finished eating, Joy poked about, looking for dessert. "I thought you and Uncle Jake were going to make a pie."

Shelby explained about Gram Kate giving the pie away.

"And you didn't say anything?" A snicker escaped Paula. "I can see Jake trying to figure out what became of his pie."

"There's more berries in here," Joy announced. She was standing before the open refrigerator, scanning the shelves for something sweet. "You could make another one."

"If I had time, I could," Shelby said. "But I'd like get on the road."

"Uncle Jake'll live, I guess," Joy concluded. She opened a package of store-bought cookies, and blurted, "Hey, I know! Take 'em to Emmie. The berries, I mean."

"Emmaline Newton. Her uncle owns Newt's Market," Paula explained at Shelby's questioning glance.

"Emmie keeps the pastry counter stocked. She also takes baking orders on the side."

Pleased at the thought of sparing Jake disappointment, Shelby said, "I'll call her, then. Thank you, Joy. That's a great idea."

Shelby phoned the store and made arrangements to drop the berries by the store on her way out of town. Paula trailed her to the car and hugged her goodbye. Joy let a casual wave suffice, then trotted after her mother, coaxing for permission to walk over to the Wiseman's house and collect her pay.

Chapter Nine

Emmaline Newton was a pert, petite young woman in her late twenties. She held up the plastic bag, squinted as she estimated how many berries it contained, then wrinkled her freckled nose. "You're short at least a cup. Two would be closer."

Having put her hand to the plow, Shelby was unwilling to abandon the idea. After all that Jake had done for her, it was a small enough matter to find her way back to the berry patch and pick a few berries for him.

"I'll leave these with you, and be back with more in a little while," she told Emmie, and took the road to Wildwood.

Once there Shelby made the solitary jaunt along the creek, over the bridge and across the field. She stopped at the first berry patch. It was one she and Jake had abandoned the evening before because of the unpleasant odor. The smell was even more overpowering today. But the berries were plump and ripe, and easily accessible.

Shelby unfolded the paper sack Emmie had given her, waded deeper into the berry bushes and tripped over a shoe. The shoe, on second glance, was attached to a foot, the foot to a leg. The leg wasn't moving. Flies swarmed. The body was...

Jake was in the boom truck, on his way to Peoria when he answered his cell phone. It took him a moment to recognize Shelby's broken babbling. When he did, his blood went cold.

"Shelby? Slow down. I can't understand you," he cried.

"He's not moving," she wailed.

"Who isn't moving?"

" I think he's... I know he's..."

"Shelby! Where are you?"

"Where we picked berries. He's dead."

"Dead? Who?"

"I don't know, I don't know. I tripped over...oh, Jake. What if he's been...I don't know...what do I..."

"He didn't hurt you?"

"No! I told you, he's dead!"

"Okay. Calm down, Shelby. Are you calling from your car?"

"Yes," she sobbed. "Near the creek."

"Stay put. I'll call 911 and be there as soon as I can."

"Hurry, Jake. Please hurry."

Heart pounding, ears roaring, Jake took her cell number, called the authorities, then called her back and stayed on the line until the police arrived.

The county sheriff came and then the coroner. The sheriff was accompanied by a female deputy, who stayed in the car with Shelby. Shelby battled for composure as she explained how she had found the body. Even as she spoke, she couldn't stop thinking about the similarity between reality and the story scene she had polished that morning.

What if it was Joy's boss, Mr. Wiseman? Fresh tears burned her eyes. *Not him. Please, God.*

"You say you were here last evening?" The deputy passed her a tissue.

Shelby nodded and dried her eyes. Tears brimmed again as she explained about bypassing the first berry patch and why. There was just no escaping the shock of finding a dead man.

Shelby's relief at Jake's arrival was overwhelming. She burst into fresh tears the moment he opened the car door. "You okay?" he asked, his face rigid with concern.

"What if it's Mr. Wiseman?" she whimpered and clutched his reaching hands with icy fingers.

"They don't know yet?"

"If they do, they haven't told me. But if it is..."

"Wait and see," he soothed. But his eyes, as he helped her from the car, reflected her own half-formed conviction.

"Joy...she tried and tried...we could have..." Shelby couldn't finish.

"Take it easy," Jake murmured. His face blurred before her tear-swollen eyes as he gathered her in. He rocked her in his arms, stroking her back, whispering words of comfort. He smelled of sunshine and soap and life. Unable to stop shaking, she clung to him and wept openly.

"Would it be all right if I took her home?" Jake asked the deputy.

The deputy asked her superior, then granted permission.

Jake drove Shelby's car back to town. Her things were in the back seat. He left them there, kept his arm around her on the way to the house, and put the teakettle on to boil. He dropped a tea bag into a cup and grabbed the kettle before it whistled.

Shelby couldn't get the tea past her swollen throat. But the cup was warm and solid and comforting between her hands.

Jake settled on the living room sofa beside her. "You never did say what you were you doing out there. When I left this morning, you were all set to go home."

"They cut your pie," she said, and explained brokenly about Gram giving the remainder to his sister Christine.

"You were going to make another one?" Surprised, and touched, Jake remarked, "You'd go to all that trouble for me?"

"I wasn't going to bake it. The girl at the store was," Shelby told him. "Emmaline. She said I needed more berries."

"It was a nice thought," Jake said, his voice low and soothing. "I'm sorry it turned out so badly."

She shuddered. Careful not to jostle hands cupping hot tea, Jake put his arm around her.

Fresh tears rose to her eyes. "Jake? I need to know if it's... Who it is and what happened to him?"

"I'll drive back out there and talk to the police," he offered. "Will you be all right here alone?"

Shelby nodded. He came to his feet. Feeling bereft, she set her tea down and reached quickly for his hand. "Thanks, Jake."

He squeezed her slim white fingers, still warm from the cup. "I'll be back as soon as I can. Paula's in the shop, if you need anything."

The news beat Jake back to town. Joy's freckles stood out like knots on her pale face as she burst into the house.

"Oh, Shelby. It's just awful. Mr. Wiseman's dead!"

Joy buried her hands in her face and spilled a broken tale of being on the doorstep of the Wiseman house when the police came and gave Mrs. Wiseman the tragic news.

"I knew it," Joy sobbed. "All along, I just knew something was wrong, that Mr. Wiseman wasn't coming back."

"You'd already spoken to Mrs. Wiseman when the police came?" Shelby asked hesitantly.

"Yes. She said she had tried to call Mr. Wiseman a couple of times while she was away on business. Then she got home and his van was there, but he wasn't." Joy crowded words, one over the other. "When I told her I hadn't seen him in three days, she got really upset. She was inside, dialing the police when they came."

Jake returned as Joy was wrapping up her account. Joy flew into his arms. Retelling the story seemed to help her. Just as she was pulling herself together, Paula came in. Joy turned into her embrace and burst into a fresh storm of tears.

Jake took Shelby to one side, and told her quietly that the police had found a bicycle. Apparently, Mr.

Wiseman had ridden out to the berry patch, left the bike by a foot path, and died as he was picking berries.

"According to Mrs. Wiseman, he had a heart condition. She wants to be sure, though, and requested an autopsy," he concluded.

Poor woman. Shelby could only imagine what she must be going through. A nasty accusation whispered that without knowing anything of Mr. Wiseman's true character she had assigned him the role of villain and had cold-bloodedly written him off at the keyboard. Stricken, she slipped upstairs to the guest room, pulled a rocking chair to the window and scanned the room for a book. Any book.

Catching herself at it, Shelby hugged her knees to her chest and denied herself the comfort of that makeshift lap she had so often curled into as a child when her father was away nipping and tucking and her mother was busy making the city a better place for those less fortunate. She couldn't escape this. She had to face it squarely.

Jake grew concerned when an hour had passed and Shelby hadn't returned downstairs. He knocked at the guest room door, then let himself in and crossed to the window where she sat huddled in the rocking chair. The late-afternoon sun caught fire in her hair and showered stark light over her tear-ravaged face.

"How's Joy?" she murmured, lowering her face.

"Cried out. Paula took her home. How about you?" he asked, heart going out to her.

Unable to find words for her remorse, Shelby knotted the damp hanky. Fresh tears pressed for release.

"I can drive you home, if you're not feeling up to it," he offered.

"I don't think so."

"You don't want to go home?"

It wasn't a matter of choice. It was unfinished. How could she pick up and go home now? *As if Mr. Wiseman's life were a story she had bungled and could not finish.*

Shelby hung her throbbing head. Jake hunkered down in front of the rocking chair. He patted her knee and squeezed her hand. His silent sympathy reminded her of Henry, the old gentleman gardener who buried her kitten when she was small.

"Once, Dad took me to get a kitten," Shelby said when the silence grew heavy. "There were two to choose between, and I couldn't decide. Dad was in a hurry, so we took them both."

"What did you name them?" Jake asked, encouraged that her thoughts had momentarily shifted from Mr. Wiseman's demise.

"Kitten names," Shelby replied, for her carelessness had cost one kitten its life even before she had settled on names. "I was supposed to keep them in the backyard. I didn't, and one was hit by a passing car."

"That happens," said Jake.

Mutely, she nodded, all the while remembering her mother's stricken, "I *told* you to keep those kittens in the fence! See what happens when you don't listen?"

They should have listened to Joy. Maybe if they'd listened…if they'd looked, Mr. Wiseman would be in the hospital instead of… Shelby said brokenly, "I'll st-stay until after the funeral."

At Jake's silence, she lifted hot eyelids. "If that's all right with you."

"You're welcome. You know that," Jake told her, wanting her to stay, and yet knowing it would make matters harder on her emotionally. "I just thought you'd made up your mind to go."

"A man died."

"I'm sorry it was you who found him. But Shelby, no one expects you to change your plans for a man you didn't know," he said gravely.

"I wrote about him," she confessed, dabbing at her eyes.

"Used him for inspiration, you mean?"

His words passed right over her head. Her aching eyes swelled again. "In my story...I was so... cavalier."

He hunkered down before the rocking chair and caught her hands in his. "Turn off the wheels for a while," he urged. "Come downstairs. I'll start supper. You can help, if you like."

"I try not to write things that...you know, might have a negative impact on young readers," Shelby continued, following her own dogged train of thought.

"Of course not. That's what I'd expect of you. I knew the moment we met that you had a good heart," he said, little knowing that his kindness only made her feel worse.

"Life is precious. But I devalued it. I did, Jake." She struggled, words catching in her throat. "Last night I asked God for a sign, and today, I find M-Mr. W-i-s-s-e-m-m-an...." Her voice broke.

"What kind of a sign?" he asked.

"…is that?" She anticipated his meaning. "I know. That's what I'm saying."

"No, I mean why were you asking for a sign? About what?" Jake asked.

His calm question logjammed thought waves. She hadn't asked concerning her writing. She had asked what to do about Jake. *And God sent her stumbling over a dead man.*

It washed over her again in a wave of near-physical illness. Reality and her story world had converged. She had lost her internal compass. She didn't know straight up anymore. "You read it, Jake."

"Your story?" he said, surprised.

"Yes, my story."

"Won't it weaken your motivation to…"

"…finish it? It doesn't matter now."

"Why not?" he asked, shifting to his feet as she rose to hers.

"Read it, Jake. Then you'll understand."

Jake accompanied her downstairs. Guilty over earlier trespasses, he stood silent as she brought up her file and scrolled to the last scene.

A muscle twitched in his jaw.

"I'll be in the kitchen," she said and turned away.

"Wait a second, don't go," he urged, and caught her hand to keep her from leaving. She tipped her face. Her red-rimmed eyes were so trusting, he lost his courage to confess and amended, "Let's read it together, okay?"

Fresh tears shimmered. She pressed fingertips to her trembling lips. "I can't, Jake. I can't make myself do it. You read it," she said, and fled, leaving him alone with her story.

Chapter Ten

In the kitchen, Shelby turned idle hands into busy ones, the long-touted panacea for all that ailed. But her strength was riddled with holes through which the darkness crept. She cried to God, and His written word echoed back a familiar promise: "Yea though I walk through the valley of the shadow of death, thou art with me."

She let the verse and the ones that followed flow through her until the rushing quieted and she could hold an ingredient list in mind long enough to retrieve shrimp, mushrooms and fresh vegetables from the refrigerator. Deveining the shrimp, she hugged close the picture of a shepherd comforting a lamb with the touch of his staff. She cleaned the vegetables, capped some mushrooms and was putting rice on to cook when the phone rang.

Jake must have answered, for it didn't ring again. Failing to find a wok, she heated olive oil in a black iron skillet instead. Her stir-fry over rice was almost ready to be served when Jake joined her in the kitchen.

"That was Wendy on the phone," he told her, and crossed to the sink to wash his hands. "She and Homer are going to pick up Gram at Rosewood and take her to dinner and a quilt exhibit downtown before bringing her home."

Shelby passed him a hand towel, and waited. But he offered nothing concerning her story. "Did you read it?" she ventured at length.

"Yes."

"And?" Shelby prompted, anxious for his opinion.

"I like your style."

"That isn't what I meant."

"I know," Jake said. He returned Gram's plate to the cupboard and her cutlery to the drawer. They clanged in the silent kitchen like a tinny piano. "Let's have dinner and then we can talk about it."

"I don't feel much like eating," Shelby admitted, peace seeping away.

"Humor me, then. I don't want to eat alone."

At a loss to deny him, Shelby iced the tea. He poured while she drained rice into a cobalt-blue dish, then seasoned the shrimp and vegetables with fresh herbs.

Jake seated her at one end of the long table and took the corner chair. He caught her cold hand in his. Shelby waited for the blessing. When none was forthcoming, she turned to meet his blue gaze.

"Gram's not here to orchestrate. You take a turn," he urged.

"I don't know if I can," she admitted.

"Sure you can," he said gently. "It'll do your heart good."

Shelby swallowed a painful knot and bowed her head. "Dear Heavenly Father…" The lump grew in her throat. She pressed her lips together, released them and tried again. "Dear Lord…" But the lump swelled and escaped in a sob. "Oh, God, what a dreadful day!"

Self-accusations swamped her again like angry seas. She pushed her plate aside and buried her face in her hands. "I never should have used him in my story."

Jake got up and returned to the table with a tissue. He pressed it into her hand, hunkered down beside her and patted her knee.

"You know what your problem is? You take your work too seriously."

"That isn't it at all!" Shelby cried, stung. "Don't you see? I didn't even know him and I played with his life."

"You played with a pretend character, Mr. Weedman," Jake said with a calmness that left her voice hanging like a shriek. "You didn't intend Mr. Wiseman any malice."

"But he died!"

"Yes he did and I'm sorry. But it isn't as if fact followed fiction. Shelby, it's likely he was dead even before Joy dropped the idea for the story into your head," Jake reasoned.

"You can't know that!"

"Not for sure, not yet anyway," he admitted. "But surely you don't have to wait for autopsy results to see that your story had nothing to do with his death."

"I wished I'd stayed home," she cried. "I never should have come here."

"So why did you?" Jake saw an open door and took it.

"The cabin was all arranged. Things fell apart, but I still...I had writing to do."

"To hide yourself in, don't you mean?" he challenged.

Injured, she defended, "Writing takes solitude. The words don't flow onto the page without some thought and effort."

"I won't venture what it does or doesn't take. All I'm saying is, it shouldn't empty you until there's nothing left for living."

"It doesn't," she said with more heat than intended.

Jake withdrew his hands and turned them palms up. His shoulders rose and fell, too.

"What?" she demanded, though he hadn't spoken.

"I'm beginning to see what your Patrick was up against."

"Patrick?" Startled, she blinked bleary eyes. "What does he have to do with anything?"

"Just about everything, if you loved the guy."

A pulse throbbed in her throat. Heat swept up already flushed cheeks. "That's what you think? That I've taken my hurt over him and used Mr. Wiseman as an excuse to have a good cry?"

"You haven't *used* Mr. Wiseman. You found him. That's your only part in what happened to Mr. Wiseman."

"But Jake, if that were true..."

"It *is* true," Jake said. "A good cry never hurt anyone. Then again, it won't do a lick of good if you turn around and bury yourself so deeply in work, you can't see what's behind the tears.''

"I know you mean well. So I'll just pretend I didn't hear that,'' Shelby snapped, trying hard not to be offended.

"Maybe you need to hear it. Don't get me wrong, I'm not finding fault,'' Jake continued hastily. "All I'm saying is it looks to me like Patrick caught you with your armor down and you ducked out. About the time you were ready to go home and take stock, Mr. Wiseman's death triggered all the stuff you buried. You came unstrung and now you can't face going home.''

"That isn't true!'' She jumped to her own defense. "I had every intention of going home before I... And I'm *not* unstrung.''

"I've got bad news, then. Your face is leaking.'' He caught a tear on his fingertip and held it up as evidence.

"It could be I was wrong about you,'' Shelby said, wounded. "I thought you were sweet.''

"I am. On you,'' he admitted.

"Oh, Jake!'' she murmured, defensiveness melting as she saw it from his point of view. "I'm sorry.''

"Don't be. You're the one with the hole in your heart.'' Hunkered down beside her chair, Jake tucked a curl behind her ear, traced the tear track and then her bottom lip with the flat of his thumb.

Shelby trapped his hand with both of hers. But it was a poor defense mechanism, for he let her keep it, leaned in and stole a kiss. It sparked heat lightning across the stormy expanse of her heart. Fiercely, she blinked tear-shine, crowded out rational thought and kissed him back. A hard, open-eyed kiss.

Jake tasted anger and hurt and despair and defiance all wrapped up in a pair of tear-salted lips. Undone, he didn't care why she kissed him, just that she did. He drew a ragged breath. "Come here," he said, his voice reduced to a whispered growl.

Wonder of wonders, she did. To her feet and into his arms. Matched him kiss for bottled-up kiss, the hunger of despair. He was searching his soul for the Pause button, when abruptly, she found it of her own accord. Her glistening forehead sagged against his chin.

"What am I doing?" she murmured, "Jake, I don't—"

Certain how the sentence would end, he said against her mouth, "I know. It's all right."

"This isn't fair to you. Forgive me," she whispered.

"Forget it," he murmured, and kissed her again and put the sensation of soft plush lips to memory. "You went to a lot trouble fixing dinner, now it's getting cold." He let her go, rather than to have her pull away on her own. Fighting to stabilize his own emotions, he forced a logic he was far from feeling, and continued, "We'll eat, then I'll take you home."

"I'm staying for the funeral, remember?" she told him.

"There isn't going to be one, Shelby."

She blinked. "There isn't?"

"Just private graveside services. That's the way Mrs. Wiseman wants it," Jake told her.

"But if there's no funeral, where is the closure?"

"For who?" he asked.

The question jerked her up short. What was she out to prove, finding reasons to stay? To whom? And to what end? Cognitive of all Jake could have said and had not, she flushed and murmured, "Point taken. I'll probably thank you later for booting me out."

"I'm not booting," he protested.

"Yes, you are, and you're right to."

"How about a rain check, then?" he asked. "For when you…"

"Bury my baggage?" she said in a voice that turned it into a loaded question.

The ringing doorbell spared Jake a response. He excused himself to answer it. It was just as well. Shelby winced to find her raw edges showing again. She climbed the stairs to splash her face and eyes in cool water and reason with herself. Home wasn't a sentence to dread. She would face down her fears and tears. Let the hurt settle, and when it had, appraise the damage. Surely nothing was broken that God couldn't fix. On that faith-based hope, Shelby collected her composure and returned to find Jake alone in the kitchen. There was a pie on the table. It was even prettier than the one he had made.

"Emmaline?" she asked.

"Now there's a woman who can bake a pie," he said.

Seeing through his banter, Shelby rewarded his effort with a watery smile. "I wonder what she did for berries."

"Used her noggin and opened a can," he replied. "I'll pay her on my way out of town."

"I took care of it. Get some pie plates. We'll have dessert first. Or has that already been served?"

Shelby colored at his gentle teasing and murmured, "You tell me."

"It has, and pie is poor seconds." He cocked his head, boyishly bold and quipped, "Nudge my memory—where were we?"

"About to eat," said Shelby.

"Oh, that. It's coming back now." He took the chair beside her. Reached for her hand and bowed his head. "We have a long drive ahead of us, and the day's about gone. But thank You for supper, and for the hands that prepared it. For the pie, too, and the thought behind it. Amen."

"Are you relaying information or is that grace?" Shelby asked.

"A little of both."

"I'll put your mind at ease, then." She collected the tattered shreds off her common sense and her pride. "I don't need a driver. I know the way home."

"Good. Then you won't have any trouble finding your way back," he countered.

Shelby looked up from smoothing her napkin. A grave smile lifted one corner of his mouth, punctuating his offer.

Chapter Eleven

Jake reasoned that he hadn't been smitten by Shelby long enough to be overboard. But when she had gone, his heaviness of spirit had her absence all over it. His missed shaded lip signatures on china cups. Dainty footprints in his garden. And fragrances. They had faded from his office, the guest room, and the bathroom closet where the bouquet of bath oils and powders and scented toiletries had lingered the longest. And with that fading away, his loneliness grew.

A week to the day Shelby had returned home, she remembered him with a blooming plant. It was delivered to the Bloomington sign shop by a local florist. He whistled on the ride home, and socked the plant down on the kitchen table where Shelby's thoughtfulness brightened Gram's day, too.

A thank-you card followed by mail the next day. The front of the card depicted a gardener leaning on his hoe, waiting out a summer shower in the doorway of his potting shed. A printed napkin from the Sunflower Tearoom fell out of the card as he opened it to Shelby's longhand.

Dear Jake and Gram Kate,

Thank you again for your hospitality. I can't imagine a more congenial place to spend a few days. Please pass along my greetings to the rest of your family. It was a pleasure meeting them and being so warmly accepted. Has Joy had any word from Mrs. Wiseman? Poor woman. She has been in my thoughts and prayers, as have both of you. Should business bring you to the city, Jake, don't forget my dinner invitation. Or if that won't work, then how about lunch? There is a tearoom on Ogden Avenue near my building you might enjoy. They serve their sandwiches on toasted sunweed seed buns. Or is that sun*flower* seed?

Cordially,
Shelby

Jake chuckled at the sunflower she had scribbled on the page and traced her signature. The inclusion of the napkin, the reminder about dinner, and the invitation to contact her bespoke a forward view and gave him hope that she had put Patrick behind her.

Admiring her resilience, Jake looked the card over more closely, and saw that she had boxed in his name on the gardener's hat. He tucked the small tearoom napkin into his wallet, then thumbed through the remaining mail.

Among the business envelopes was a bid request from Spot Dry Cleaning, a firm with seven stores in the Chicago area. One of the stores was on Ogden

Avenue. Jake found it midway between the tearoom and Parnell Publishing where Shelby worked.

With a glut of local work to keep his men busy, the timing wasn't the greatest. And it would mean a week or more away from home, should he get the bid.

Jake weighed the pros and cons briefly, and reached for his calendar. He would have to survey the job before making a bid. It would take a full day. He was looking for one he could free up when Joy burst into his office.

"You'll never guess who I heard from," she cried, her eyes shining like northern lights.

"Dirk?" Jake took a stab in the dark.

"Not on the phone, e-mail! Go on, guess!"

Jake circled a calendar date in red, twisted his mouth to one side and asked, "How about a hint?"

"He has his own Web site. I saw it in a magazine, and sent him an e-mail. But he must not check his mail much, because it took me a long time to hear back," Joy continued.

"You call that a hint?" asked Jake.

"Okay, I'll just tell you. Are you ready for this? Ta-da!" Joy exclaimed with all the grandeur of an unveiling, and thrust an e-mail from Colton under Jake's nose.

Flowers and a bread-and-butter note elicited no response from Liberty Flats. Not that Shelby had expected word. The silence, not to mention the passing days, enabled her to view Mr. Wiseman's death with less trauma and more insight.

She was plotting another book to replace the one

she had left unfinished when Joy e-mailed her, asking if she wanted her to delete her story from Jake's files.

Shelby replied by e-mail that she had already done so.

Joy responded swiftly: "But I thought you wanted me to do it, once you made sure you had received it at home."

Shelby felt no obligation to explain how in one ill-fated moment, the story had become a brick wall she couldn't seem to find passage over, under or through. She closed the subject with a few tactful words and sent her warm regards to the rest of the family.

Once again, days passed with no word. Shelby dug into her work. But her new story, begun with promise, soon fizzled out like a wet firecracker.

Stuck, she buried herself in indexing a cookbook. The associate editor who had begun the indexing was on maternity leave, so it had fallen to Shelby. It was mundane and tedious eye-straining work, her least favorite of jobs. So much so, that when the phone rang one evening as she was pouring over the pages she had brought home from work, she welcomed the interruption. It was a heartbeat past hello when she recognized Patrick's voice. For one unguarded moment, the hurt crowded in.

"I hope I didn't catch you at a bad time," he began.

"Not at all. How have you been?" she said, thinking it pointless to ignore the ashes.

"Fine, thanks. And you?" asked Patrick.

"The same."

"I suppose your writing is keeping you busy," he ventured.

"As always," she agreed, but surprisingly, felt no

desire to offer the particulars as she once would have done.

Patrick cleared his throat and stated the purpose of his call. He had been contacted by Parnell Publishing concerning a potential lawsuit. "Apparently Miss Lockwood doesn't like the cover on her book."

Well aware of the situation, Shelby replied, "She liked it well enough to sign off on it. It's too late to change her mind now."

"I seem to recall an earlier snag—some careless-ness in her research, wasn't it?"

"It was a book about traveling in Canada. Very warm and user friendly. But in one instance, some descriptive details were almost a mirror image to those in a Canadian travel brochure," Shelby ex-plained, recovering her ease as it dawned it was busi-ness, not personal matters, that had prompted the call.

"As I recall, it was you who caught it," Patrick was saying.

"She knows that," countered Shelby.

"It wouldn't hurt to refresh her memory."

"Apply a little pressure, you mean?"

"It would be a kindness, Shelby," Patrick contin-ued. "She's obviously not thinking this through. If she were, she would be busy writing her next book instead of threatening a suit she can't win. Will you join us for lunch tomorrow?"

"No, thank you, I'd rather not," Shelby replied, shrinking at the thought.

"And here I thought you were a team player," coaxed Patrick.

"I must be, or I wouldn't be taking my work home

with me every night. And with a book of my own to worry about,'' she returned.

"Excuse me, Shelby, but I have an interruption on my hands," Patrick said. "Rethink lunch, and I'll call you back."

Shelby fidgeted and couldn't get back into her work for second-guessing herself. There had to be a first time of seeing him again. Perhaps after that, it would grow easier to relegate the past to the past, and view him simply as a lawyer Parnell Publishing had retained to handle a legal matter. On the other hand, why should she subject herself to a potentially uncomfortable scene, both in the social and business sense, just to make his job easier? There was something very liberating in her reluctance to do so. It was freeing, too, that the thunder in her ears at the sound of his voice had quickly faded to a distant echo.

Empowered by the realization her heart was on the recovering list, she waited expectantly for him to call back, and when the phone rang, lifted the receiver from the cradle with hard-fought confidence. "I've thought it over, and the answer's still no," she said without preamble.

"Shelby?"

"I've done my part, and I have nothing further to contribute. That's why they contacted you." Shelby held her firm line, giving him no chance to squeeze in a word.

"Here I thought it was because I can spell *spot*."

Confused, Shelby grappled to identify the familiar voice.

"It's Jake," he volunteered. "Did I catch you in the middle of something?"

"Jake! I'm sorry! I was expecting a return call, and I thought—" Shelby caught herself up short. "What do you mean, you can spell *spot?*"

"Spot Dry Cleaning," Jake said. "I'll be in town tomorrow to bid on a job for them."

"*That* Spot!" said Shelby, getting a grip. "They have a store not far from where I work."

"Yes, I know. Are you free for lunch?" Jake asked.

"Yes, and it's my treat," she reminded.

"I got your potted plant. Thanks, that was thoughtful."

"I'm glad you liked it. Is it still blooming?" she asked.

"Most of the petals have faded, but the greenery is nice. Gram is enjoying it, too. About this tearoom—will I be needing a tux?" he quipped.

An image of Jake climbing out of his crane truck dressed in a tuxedo, work boots and a Jackson Signs cap flitted through her mind. She smiled and said, "You'd feel a little out of place, it's casual. Even better, it's within walking distance for me."

"I'm sold. What time?"

"We can beat the rush if we are there by eleven-thirty. Can you make that?" she asked.

"I'll try. You'll be the lady in the sunflower dress?"

"I could be." Looking forward to seeing him again, she twisted the phone cord around her finger and asked, "How have you been?"

"Busy playing catch-up. We had electrical storms and high winds a week ago," he told her.

"I guess that *would* be a boon to the sign industry."

Jake chuckled agreement and went on to ask her if she had replaced her car. She had. Her computer had proved a fatality, as well. Having learned of it through his insurance man, Jake asked if she had had any problems replacing it. Expected call forgotten, Shelby told him all about it. He in turn shared that Joy had received a nice note and a check from Mrs. Wiseman for the hours she had spent weeding fields for Mr. Wiseman.

"That's good, I'm glad to hear it," said Shelby. "She was pleased, I'm sure."

"Oh, yes. She put on her apron in celebration, and was all set to try baking a pie when she got sidetracked."

"What? A butter bean cake recipe?"

"No, the computer. She came across a Web page for Wind, Sky and Water. Being her usual resourceful self, she got from that to an e-mail address for The Voyager."

"She contacted her father?" gasped Shelby. "Does Paula know?"

"Yes. He called to check out Joy's story."

"What did she tell him?"

"The truth," Jake replied. "Right away, he asked to see Joy."

Clearly, Colton's phone call had caused everyone involved emotional upheaval, Jake included. "Did Paula agree?" she asked.

"Only to think about it. For Joy's sake," he added.

His somber tone was in sharp contrast to the bantering tone on which their conversation had begun. Shelby listened, breath caught, as he expressed Paula's concern over Colton having the means to pursue and no doubt win visitation rights, if he so chose. Joy was pressuring Jake to intervene on her behalf and Paula was counting on him to back her up in whatever decision she made. Jake didn't belabor being the man in the middle except to say, tongue in cheek, he was starting to envy Gram in her friction-free world of forgetfulness.

Curious though she was about Colton, Paula and Joy, Shelby didn't want to add to his burden by asking a lot of questions. "How is Gram Kate?"

"Pretty fit, all things considered. We're planning a birthday party for her on the Saturday before Labor Day," he said on a brighter note. "Are you free?"

"Hold on a moment and I'll check." Before Shelby could change to a phone in reach of her calendar, she was signaled by Call Waiting. "Jake? Could I let you know tomorrow? I have another call."

Jake agreed and said goodbye.

It was Patrick, calling back. Shelby felt childish for that momentary lift it gave her to tell him that she had plans for lunch tomorrow and wouldn't be free. Patrick reacted graciously, which wasn't nearly so deflating as it might have been. Repenting of her shallow pride, she prayed for Jake's family. Obviously, what Joy had begun with an e-mail had ramifications she wouldn't know to consider.

Shelby wrapped up the indexing work she had brought home from the office with her, and filled the tub. As she soaked in rose-scented water, her thoughts turned once more to Jake. Looking forward to seeing him, and wanting to look her best, she toweled off, and padded to her closet to lay out clothes for the next day. She deliberated over the yellow

pleated dress, then discarded Jake's broad hint as too
casual for the office.

The wedding dress was still in the closet, and still
in the way. Shelby thumbed past it for a pale-green
linen suit and in so doing, realized all that white satin
and lace had lost its bite. Behind the suit was a
blouse she had bought on sale the previous summer.

It was white silk, with narrow mist-green edging
along the button flap. Shelby hung both to one side,
and the next morning, found the results pleasing. Lingering in front of the mirror, she ran a comb through
her curls and made a mental note to call her stylist.

Jake was on the road before daylight the next
morning. He stopped for breakfast midway to the
city, and reached the first of seven dry cleaning es-
tablishments just as the manager arrived. He measured the existing signs, snapped pictures for docu-
mentation, drove to two more locations to repeat the
procedure, then made his way back to Ogden Avenue
to meet Shelby for lunch.

The tearoom was on the ground floor of a turn-of-
the-century building. Bronze gaslight fixtures hung
from a high tin ceiling. The gas mantels had been
replaced by soft pink bulbs concealed in tulip-shaped
stained-glass shades. The tables were covered in an-
tique-white linen and lighted by reproduction Tiffany
lamps.

A greeter led him past a wall lined in tea sets to
a little built-in nook where Shelby sat looking over
typewritten pages. He had almost reached the booth
when she lifted her head from her work. Recognition
flashed in her eyes, and warmed her whole face.

"Hello, Jake," she said, and folded her glasses

away. "I hope you didn't have trouble finding the place?"

"No. Traffic slowed me down. Sorry I'm late." He slid into the upholstered seat to share the same side of the table, and retrieved a small sack from his shirt pocket. "I found something for you when we stopped for breakfast this morning."

The sack, printed in a floral design, was no bigger than an index card. Shelby reached inside and peeled back tissue paper, revealing a ceramic tea bag holder with yellow petals flaring out from a brown center. "A sunflower. Thank you, Jake."

"Sunweed," he corrected with a grin.

"That's right, I keep forgetting." Shelby scanned his face, searching for telltale signs of weariness and stress. But he appeared relaxed and pleased to see her. She started to ask about Paula, then changed her mind, thinking he would bring up the subject himself if he wanted to talk about it.

"There's a pie pan and a rolling pin to match," Jake said, as she neatly folded the pretty gift sack into her pocketbook. "They were a little bulky. I left them in the truck."

"You'd better take them home to Joy," she said, and wrinkled her nose, admitting, "as a pie baker, I'm a lost cause."

"Here I thought I was a good teacher," he said.

Shelby flushed at his reference to that moment in the kitchen, and welcomed the interruption the waitress provided as she arrived to take their order. She chose cranberry tea for her beverage and when it was served, put her gift to use. Cranberry-tinted tea spread over the ceramic flower.

"A sunflower with pinkeye," observed Jake.

"Is there a physician in the house?" She played along. Following his lead, she kept the conversation general as they waited for their food.

Shelby's spinach salad was more than she needed. She shared it with Jake. In turn, he lobbed off a piece of his sandwich and insisted she try it. The sandwich, smoked ham with a specialty dressing, was tucked between crusty bread and topped in toasted sunflower seeds.

"Very good," she said, smoothing her napkin.

"The salad, too," Jake agreed. "You can take me out anytime."

Shelby smiled and nibbled on a pickle. "Will you be in the city a few days?"

"No. I'll start home as soon as I've checked out the other dry cleaning locations."

"And if you get the bid? When will you be back?" asked Shelby.

"I'm guessing late August," he said.

"Call and let me know, and we'll get together again, if you like."

"I like." Jake smiled, savoring the lushness of her eyes, the hue, the thick fringe of lashes. Just the way he remembered. There was a difference, though. Subtle enough, he kept searching.

"Where's your sunflower dress?" he asked.

"I'm saving it for Gram Kate's birthday party."

"You've cleared your calendar, then?" He watched her over the rim of his coffee cup.

"I have. And I'm looking forward to seeing everyone."

"Have you done something different with your hair?"

A faint blush rose to her cheeks at his lingering

scrutiny. "It's a little long. I've been meaning to make an appointment for a cut."

"It looks nice," he said.

She tucked an errant curl behind her ear, so feminine a gesture. Seemingly of its own volition, his arm draped the seat back behind her. "How's the book coming?"

"The Weed Buster's thing?" She wrinkled her nose but didn't shirk the featherlight touch of his fingers skimming her shoulder. "It isn't."

"What's the problem?" he asked.

"I can't get past the field scene. And I can't take it out. If I do, the plot falls apart," Shelby explained.

"Can't you rewrite the scene?"

"If only I could. But even the thought of trying..." She shrugged and fell short of explaining.

"Oh, go ahead. Bend my ear," he said and leaned closer.

Shelby reached up and patted his ear.

His fingers trapped hers as he cupped the ear she had touched on a whim. "I can't hear you," he said, cradling her hand.

"I don't want to talk about it," she said.

"You'll feel better," he coaxed.

"No, I won't," she said, distracted by his fingers loosely laced with hers. "I told you, when I talk it out, I lose my incentive to—"

"I've already read your story," he reasoned. "So, what's at stake?"

His eyes, so sky-blue earnest, coaxed to light an unvoiced fear that she had lost her first love. Her muse. Her writing. It was a worry she hadn't whispered, not even to God.

She withdrew her hand and settled for half measures, saying, "I've taken the scene apart in my mind more times than I can count. It starts out okay. My characters react strongly. But only for a sentence or so, and then they carry on as if..."

"As if, what?" he prompted when she hesitated.

"As if Mr. Weedman's death doesn't matter beyond giving them a fright."

"And it does."

"Of course it does," she said with quiet conviction. "In their shoes, I was terrified. Sick. It was like someone else reacting from within my skin. I don't know how else to explain it. I still dream about it." Her voice fell. Her lashes swept up in silent inquiry.

"So convey the loss," he said. "You can do it."

When he put it that way, she yearned to rise to the occasion. Because she thought she could succeed where she had thus far failed? Or because she wanted to please him? As with the pie, and even in her care not to speak of Paula's problems, unless he was willing to bring it up himself. What was it about him that made her so eager to accommodate?

The waitress came with strawberries and scones and distracted Shelby from sorting it out. She hadn't ordered dessert. At her wordless glance, Jake shrugged to say he hadn't, either.

"It looks good, but I'm afraid you have the wrong table," Shelby began.

"Compliments of Mr. Delaney. He'd like you to stop by his table when you've finished eating." The waitress indicated a table nearby.

Shelby turned to see Patrick and a striking redhead seated there. Monique Lockwood. Shelby hadn't met her in person. But she recognized the author's profile from the photo on the book jacket, one of several she had submitted throughout the editorial process.

"A work associate," she answered Jake's questioning glance.

He heard the brittle note and drew his own conclusions.

Shelby fumed in silence over the unfair advantage Patrick had taken in knowing her daily patterns, right down to her favorite lunch spot. What did he hope to accomplish? If Miss Lockwood's discontent could have been resolved by Parnell staff, he wouldn't have been called in.

"I'm sorry, I didn't save room," she said to the waitress, waiving dessert.

"Sir?" said the waitress to Jake.

"No, thanks. Do you have our check?"

The waitress tallied their ticket and gave it to Jake. Shelby avoided looking Patrick's way again. But his table was in direct line with the door. She wiped the tea bag holder dry, tucked it into her book bag and excused herself to freshen up.

Jake stood up and let her out. "I'll wait for you up front," he said, and strode for the register, tab in hand.

Shelby ducked into the powder room, made short work with comb and lipstick and let herself out again. As she neared Patrick's table, the waitress served their meal and strode away. Shelby closed the remaining distance, intending to say, Hello-how-are-you-Don't-let-your-food-get-cold-Goodbye. But before she could, Patrick reached for Miss Lockwood's hand. It startled Shelby so, she kept walking.

"Ready?" Jake asked, and held the door for her.

Shaken, she ducked under his arm and into the

noonday sun. Patrick and Monique Lockwood? Had he deceived her? No. Not Patrick. Couldn't be. Lack of wholehearted devotion, he had said. On *her* part, not his. But the possibility—it was like a firecracker going off in her mind.

Shelby unclenched her fists. She felt blood flow into her fingers. Heat radiated off brick walls and from the pavement underfoot. She tipped her head back, gazed through the porthole of tall buildings to God's sky above, emptied a caught breath and realized she was still in one piece. Seeing Patrick with another woman hadn't destroyed her. Even the tremors were quickly settling.

"Careful," warned Jake. His arm shot out to steady her as crumbling sidewalk snagged her high heel.

His hand, strong and scuffed and warm, was a welcome sensation. Shelby drew no comparisons and made no excuses for finding comfort in it. But once he had steadied her, he released her arm and looked back toward the tearoom.

"Did you forget something?" Shelby asked, pausing beside him.

"No. Just wondering about dessert."

"You mean Patrick?"

"*The* Patrick?"

She nodded. A shadow fell over his face and pinched her heart. "I'm sorry. I would have introduced you, but... It's kind of a long story. Do you have time?"

"That's up to you. It's your affair."

The edge to the word seemed premeditated. Shelby tilted her hot face and in so doing caught a glimpse of his hardened jaw. It was wounding, surprisingly so.

"Monique Lockwood has an ax to grind with Parnell Publishing." She found herself explaining. "Patrick is trying to avoid a lawsuit. Apparently he thought that my presence might be of some help."

"He works for Parnell?"

"When they need representation," Shelby said. "That's how we met."

Jake didn't pursue it. Nor did it seem likely that a rush of explanations would soften his demeanor. They passed the remaining block to her building in silence. It was deflating, that silence.

"End of the trail. This is where I work." Shelby pushed the slim strap of her pocketbook higher on her shoulder, then gripped her book bag with both hands, breath caught as she awaited his leave-taking.

"I'll let you get back to your desk," he said. "Thanks for lunch."

"Thank *you*, don't you mean?" Shelby responded, for she had intended it to be her treat before Patrick rocked the boat and rattled her senses.

Jake smiled, faint and formal, his heart all the while twisting. "It was good seeing you again."

"Me, too," she said, purse strap slipping; heart, too, at his toneless and impersonal politeness. "Give Gram Kate my love. Tell Joy hello. Paula, too."

"Will do." Jake lifted his hand and turned away without further mention of being in touch, or reiterating his invitation to Gram Kate's birthday party.

A pungent sense of loss carried her back once again to that day in the potting shed where Henry had come for a shovel to bury her kitten. She remembered his rough earthy hands as he wiped her tears and sent her inside for a shoe box and something of her own to bury with the kitten. She had returned with her favorite storybook. Henry, dear old gentle soul, had held her on his lap and read the story aloud before tucking it into the box with the kitten. Carelessness, she learned, came at a cost.

But this carelessness was not hers. It was Patrick's.

Shelby fumbled in her book bag for her keepsake. She held it aloft and called after Jake as he strode away, "Thanks for the sunflower."

There was a quiet plea in her call. Jake heard it, but didn't know how it piece it with what had happened in there. *Business?* Maybe. She didn't offer just where she stood with Patrick now, and he wouldn't ask. Couldn't, on the basis of their short acquaintance. But he had as much pride as the next man, and if it was a game she was playing trying to make her ex-fiancé jealous, she wasn't the woman he had taken her to be.

As for Spot Dry Cleaning, he'd gone to the trouble, he might as well follow through and make the bid. But if the work came his way, that's all it was. A job, and nothing more.

He climbed into his truck. The rolling pin and pie plate were in a bag on the seat beside him. Silent testimony to his weakness for her, a weakness strong enough to make him crowd out simple logic.

Hadn't he known all along that the responsibilities he shouldered didn't leave him much liberty to find someone who could fill that empty place in his life? That hadn't changed just because his feelings had. Now, it was more true than ever, what with Colton hovering like a funnel cloud from a breath-caught spring sky.

Chapter Twelve

Shelby couldn't get Jake off her mind, nor shake the sinking feeling their relationship had taken a dead end. Thanks to Patrick's little manipulation. *If you didn't know better, you'd think he had done it on purpose.*

Shelby passed the afternoon unfocused and unsettled and arrived home to a ringing phone.

"Hi, Shelby. What happened to you today?" asked Patrick. "I looked up and you were gone."

"You put me in an awkward position, *that's* what happened," said Shelby, temperature rising.

"I'm sorry. When you said you had plans for lunch, I didn't realize it was a date."

"Well, it was. And if I want dessert, I'll order it."

"Of course. Again, I apologize." He cleared his throat. "On a brighter note, Miss Lockwood has changed her mind."

Patrick's hand reaching for Monique's flashed in instant replay. Shelby resisted cross-examining the master of cross-examiners, and said nothing.

"There won't be a lawsuit," Patrick continued. "Shelby? Are you still there?"

"Yes," Shelby said. "I'm just wondering what you said to bring her to her senses."

"It wasn't what I said, it's who I represented."

Shelby assumed he meant Parnell Publishing. "So, she's having second thoughts about burning her bridges?"

"That, too," he said.

"It's a little late. Granted, she's gifted, but who needs the grief?"

"You're still angry."

I'm no longer your concern. Shelby bit her tongue to keep from reminding him.

"I guess I didn't tell you I met Monique several weeks ago," Patrick continued.

Again, she waited him out.

"At Can-Do." He shed her silence like a squeaky clean window sheeting rain. "I didn't realize at the time who she was."

"Monique Lockwood volunteers at Can-Do?"

"No. I said I met her there."

"She's on the board, then?" Shelby sought somewhat impatiently to understand. "Not the staff, surely."

"She's working through some problems."

"What are you saying? Spit it out, would you Patrick?"

"Her marriage failed. Her business, too," Patrick said. "There was no safety net to catch her."

"Monique Lockwood is *homeless?*" Thunderstruck, Shelby cried, "I can't believe it! How could she write a travel book without a corner to call her own?"

"She traveled widely before her divorce and drew from her trip journals."

"Journals?" Shelby echoed.

"And photos. Her journals and albums are just about all she came away with. After the divorce, I mean," said Patrick.

"It boggles the mind."

"Doesn't it? For a few months, she actually lived in her car," Patrick told her.

"She has a car, then?"

"She did, until the insurance and the license tags needed renewing and she didn't have the money. She sold the car, moved into the mission and continued her writing on a computer at the public library," Patrick added. "She wouldn't want her readership to know that, of course."

"Give me a little credit, would you?"

"Could I say something?" Taking her silence for consent, Patrick said, "I know you're hurting, and I'm sorry."

"That isn't fair, Patrick. I'm not hurting, and anyway, it isn't germane. We were discussing Monique," Shelby replied stiffly.

"If it's any consolation, it wasn't cold feet," he spoke over her protest.

Stung, she countered, "If it's any consolation, you were right. I didn't put you first. Today at lunch, it hit me out of the blue—I'd lost my first love."

"Oh, Shelby."

"Not you! My writing!" she cried, at his melting tone.

Silence held the moment. He sighed finally, and said, "Maybe you should check your priorities. Last I heard, God still likes to be first."

Nonplused, she demanded, "What's happened to you?"

"I came to the end of myself. Perhaps you should try it."

"Patrick Delaney! I resent that!"

"I'm wrong? Then maybe we'll run into one another at Can-Do tomorrow night," Patrick suggested.

Shelby tried to recall when she had last volunteered at the mission, and couldn't. It wasn't a deliberate omission. It was just that life over the past couple of years had become a balancing act.

"I can't. I have plans."

"A date?"

"No. I'm working late," Shelby said.

"I see," he drawled.

Loaded words, and he knew it. Shelby ended the call before she lost her grasp on civility. She paced her living room, listing all the reasons she no longer had time to sling hash or sort secondhand clothes at Can-Do. There was the cookbook bearing down on her at Parnell's. Her writing was in collapse. She didn't want to miss Jake, should he call.

Which he didn't, thanks to Patrick.

A week passed with no word. And then another. The wound inflicted by Jake's silence confused her. It's no great loss. You hardly know him, she told herself.

Her writing was no help. Jake's urging had motivated her to revive her attempts on the Weed Busters book. But she continued to hit the same stone wall. One evening, tired of listening for a phone call that wasn't going to come, Shelby locked her apartment and arrived at Can-Do just in time to help with the dishes.

The director, Mr. Weaver came in later that evening as she was hanging up her apron. He thanked her for her help, and commented that they had missed her at Can-Do. Before Shelby could explain her lack of free time, he brought her up to date on a teen program recently undertaken by the mission.

Mr. Weaver asked if she would be willing to help with an outing planned by a supporting church group for a week from Saturday. Not long ago, Shelby would have excused herself by virtue of needing the time to write. Now she agreed readily, partly to disprove Patrick's words about her priorities, partly to avoid confrontation at the keyboard.

Two weeks after submitting his bid on the Chicago job, Jake got word the work was his. He scheduled the work for the last week of August.

Changing the signs required two trucks and three men. Wendy's husband Homer, and another brother-in-law, Gordy, went along with him. Once in Chicago, they got the necessary permits, checked in with the union hall, and made good headway the first day. But the remainder of the week, Jake was faced with delays and complications, one after another.

His men wanted to spend the weekend with their families and return on Monday to complete the job. But Jake talked them into staying one more night and doing the Ogden Avenue location on Saturday. Homer drew his own conclusions.

"You going to give Shelby a jingle?" he asked, as Jake turned the crane truck back toward the motel at dusk on Friday.

"Hadn't planned on it. Why?" Jake asked.

"If you like, I could coach you on the finer points of catching a gal on the rebound," offered Homer.

Goaded, Jake replied, "Make yourself useful and crank that mirror in, would you?"

Homer reached out the passenger's window and adjusted the side mirror. "That better?"

"Can you see yourself in it?" Jake asked. "Tell me—does that look like Dear Abby to you?"

Homer cackled and said no more. He was right, though. There was the rub. Jake couldn't get Shelby off of his mind. A woman crossed his path these days, and all he saw was points of comparison. Shelby came out ahead every time. It wasn't as if he hadn't considered calling her. Truth was, he fought the temptation daily. So far, overcoming had proved a hollow victory.

The next morning, Jake and his men arrived at the Ogden Avenue location early. Using one crane to work out of and the other to lift, they had the old sign down by midmorning.

The proprietor treated them to donuts and coffee. Jake was brushing the powdered sugar off his shirt when his pulse reacted to a familiar figure climbing out of a parked car.

Shelby. It came over him like repetitive motion. Tight chest. Spitfire pulse. Misbehaving limbs wanting to angle her way instead of following his men onto the truck bed to uncrate the new sign.

Her dress was a filmy sea-green thing. The bodice was slim-fitting, the skirt was gored. The breeze filled the skirt, wafting it about her curves and slim calves like delicate sea foam. She circled to the passenger's side, leaned in and plucked something out of the seat.

Jake couldn't tell what, just that it was white and lengthy and covered in plastic. Hands full, she closed the car door with her hip and clipped along half-hidden by whatever it was that encumbered her.

She hadn't cut her hair. Red-gold curls bounced above shoulders that hadn't seen much sunlight. In a city of sun goddesses, she strolled along as creamy-white as the gown in her arms.

Wedding gown. It registered as the distance fell away. She looked so radiant in that shower of sunlight, his heart sank. His gaze went to her left hand. It was hidden in the folds of the wedding dress.

She stepped around the outrigger, set there on the sidewalk. Looked at the truck. Stopped, and for one unguarded moment let a smile blossom.

"Jake! Long time no see!" Shelby exclaimed, awash with spontaneous pleasure at the sight of him.

Her starburst greeting gave rise to all those old feelings. He'd been a fool not to call her. He crimped his hat and asked, "Working Saturdays now?"

"No. I'm running some errands," Shelby said.

"So, he changed his mind again?"

She blinked, and echoed, "Who changed his mind?"

Jake saw her ringless hand, then, and felt as transparent as the plastic covering her gown. "The weather man," he improvised, and shuffled his feet. "Early showers, he predicted. Doesn't look like showers to me, does it you?"

"I won't complain," she said and shrugged her creamy shoulders.

Jake looked over his shoulder. Homer's brother Gordy gawked and grinned. Homer parodied catching a rebound. Jake turned back, neck on fire. He indicated the gown. "So, where you headed with that?"

"The cleaners. My friends tell me it should be treated and packed away," she replied.

"What for?"

"Posterity, I guess," she said with a pretty shrug.

"Seems like a waste."

"Do you have a better idea?"

"Sure do. A better man," he suggested on inspiration.

"You should talk," she countered mildly. "You said you'd call when you came to town. You didn't. Your sign says you're working. You're not."

"What sign?"

"That sign." Her fingers wiggled free of shimmering satin. She pointed to the Men Working sign he had posted along the street.

"I was. Then you came along and distracted me," Jake replied, holding back a grin.

"I'll go, then," she said, and would have, too, except he got between her and Spot Dry Cleaner's front door.

"Have you had breakfast?" he asked.

"Yes," she replied, heart stopping as he blocked her path.

"Lunch, then?"

"It's ten o'clock, Jake. Who eats at ten?" she huffed, pride preventing her from being readily available when he had left her dangling all this time without so much as a word.

"Since when do we eat by the clock? Come on, at least have a cup of coffee with me," he coaxed, determined to make the most of what seemed to him like nothing short of divine intervention.

"I can't. I'm parked in a loading zone."

"How about noon, then?" he pressed.

"I'd like to, Jake," she admitted, yielding a bit. "But I promised I'd chaperone some kids to a Wiffle Ball game. "

"Wiffle Ball?"

"It's all the rave here in the city. They play in bumper cars. With paddles, wickets, whatever you want to call them."

"I'm intrigued," he said, and he was. With her.

A wistfulness softened her face as she reconsidered her day. "Would you like to come along?"

"Sure," Jake replied, feeling like a two-ton boulder had been lifted off him. "If I won't be intruding."

"We could use another chaperon," she said, and gave him the address.

Jake tucked it into his pocket, and reached past her to hold the door. "We'll finish up here, then I'll meet you there."

Her curls brushed his hand as she ducked under his arm. That silky sensation left a sweet ache that stayed with him throughout the morning. The sign was up and working by noon. Homer and Gordy chained down the old sign and left for home.

Jake climbed behind the wheel of the second crane truck, studied the city map a minute, and set off to meet Shelby. It was raining by the time he arrived. But the bumper car court was part of an indoor arcade, complete with video games and a miniature golf course, all under one roof. Judging by the noise, the fun was in full swing. Jake spotted Shelby resting a slender hip against the half wall that enclosed the bumper car court.

His cap, shirt and shoes were rain-spotted. But for the first time in weeks, a sunny front moved in over his heart.

Chapter Thirteen

Shelby didn't attend the church supporting the outing. She didn't know any of the kids or the other two chaperons. But all seemed to be enjoying the bumper car sport. Players, divided into teams of five, dodged and bumped and rattled about, trying to keep track of a Whiffle Ball. They used hand-held wickets to steal, to carry, and to pass as well as to score points.

Boisterous cheers chimed with the general clamor of the surrounding arcade. Shelby glanced at her watch for the third time in that many minutes, and turned to see Jake catch her at it. Their eyes met. The din fell away, muffled by the drumming in her ears as he joined her at the wall.

"Am I late?" he asked, reseating his cap.

Shelby's heart responded to the familiar gesture. "Depends on whether you want to watch or play."

"Play, of course. So what's the idea? Bumper car, basketball or baseball?" he asked, turning to watch the kids play.

"A mix, as close as I can tell," she said, and admitted she had never played herself.

"How are we going to compete if we don't know the rules?"

"I'm not," she said. "But don't let that stop you."

"Oh, come on. How hard can it be?" he cajoled. "You can drive, can't you?"

"I haven't collided with any falling cranes lately."

"Don't start with me," he said, and laughed.

Shelby wasn't sure what impulse governed her. But when the opportunity came, she climbed into one of the little cars and complicated the game. It was apparent to all she couldn't catch or throw the Wiffle Ball with any reliability. Twice, she dropped her wicket outside the car and imposed on Jake to retrieve it. But there were advantages to being unskilled. The kids took pity on her, and didn't mix it up with her the way they did with Jake. He was plainly in his element, and quickly developed a rapport with them, whistling in snatches and calling them by name.

"That your best shot, Brady?" hollered Jake, as a skinny curly-haired kid missed his shot.

"Sun was in my eyes," claimed Brady.

"What sun? It's raining out," scoffed Jake.

"So?" said Brady.

Jake chortled and dubbed him Sun-Blind Brady.

Enjoying the status derived from Jake's attention, Brady banged and bumped Jake all over the court. The other kids giggled and shrieked and joined the chase. It didn't take a high-spirited pursuit long to deteriorate into what resembled an all-out demolition derby.

All the chaos reminded Shelby why she preferred word games. She parked her car and joined the other chaperons, looking on as bumper cars converged on Jake from all directions.

"Careful, you'll hurt him!" she cried.

"You heard her—you'll hurt me," chimed Jake. He extracted himself from the melee, clamored out of his car and over the wall, and ducked behind Shelby.

Egged on by his clowning, the kids abandoned their cars and poured over the wall after him. Chaperons seized the moment and announced that it was time to leave. Amidst a chorus of protests and groans, Shelby and Jake helped get the kids lined up. The other chaperons took over, and marched their charges out into the drizzle.

Brady turned en route to the church bus. He looked back at Shelby and Jake standing beneath the portico. "Are you coming with us, Jake?"

"Thanks, Brady, but I've got my truck," Jake called back.

"Follow us, then and you can eat dinner with us."

"Like he wants to eat at the mission," muttered another boy.

Jake glanced at Shelby. He palmed his cap, rubbed the back of his neck and called after the boys, "So, what's on the menu?"

"Hamboogies," said Brady with a toothy grin. "And fries. She can eat with us, too, if she wants."

"Gee, thanks." Shelby deadpanned at his postscript inclusion of her.

Jake grinned and slipped his arm through hers. "Burgers and fries, it is."

Brady's seeking look became a smile. He turned

and climbed the bus steps backward. "I'll save you a place, Mr. Jackson. You riding back with us, ma'am?" he called to Shelby from the top step.

"She better come with me. I may need directions," Jake said quickly.

Brady accepted that as gospel and scrambled into the front seat of the bus.

"What kind of group have we got here, anyway?" Jake asked, as Shelby waved to the lively faces smiling from bus windows.

"Hope Chapel middle graders, plus some kids from Can-Do," she replied.

"Can-Do?"

"It's a homeless mission."

"Kids, living at a mission?"

"With their families," Shelby said, nodding. The drizzle was so fine, it was almost a mist. She ambled at Jake's side, crossing the parking lot to his truck, filling him in on the mission. "Most don't stay long. But, whether it's a day or several weeks, Can-Do provides a safe haven while families work through whatever life crisis put them out of house and home."

"And the outing?"

"A number of churches take turns planning outings. The idea is to give the children a break from burdens kids weren't meant to carry. Having fun with other kids is good medicine," she repeated what Mr. Weaver, the mission director, had told her about the new youth program.

"Tough circumstance for a kid to be in."

"Yes," Shelby agreed. "But they wear it well. I distributed arcade passes at the mission while we were waiting for the church bus to arrive. That's the only way I knew which children did and didn't have homes."

"It's a good thing you're doing," Jake said.

His simple earnest words fell on undeserving ears. Or so Shelby felt, as Jake unlocked his truck and held the door. Had Patrick not hit a nerve over the phone weeks earlier, it was unlikely she would be here now.

"Careful," Jake warned, and gripped her elbow to prevent her from slipping on the damp side iron.

Jake read modesty into Shelby's silence. He maneuvered the slick streets. The skies opened up, making visibility difficult for the last several blocks. Jake lost sight of the bus.

"The turnoff is just beyond the sign." Shelby directed Jake into Can-Do Mission's fenced-in parking lot.

"No need in both of us getting rained on. I'll pull up to the door and let you out," he offered.

"That's okay. Let's wait it out together," Shelby suggested, relishing his company.

Jake parked across the lot along the fence. The children disembarked at the mission door. The church bus pulled away in the driving rain.

"I've been thinking about what you said," Jake stated, lifting his voice above the clamor of the rain on the cab roof.

"About what?" Shelby asked.

"Reminding me I hadn't called."

"It's all right, Jake," Shelby murmured, faintly embarrassed by the words that had popped out at their own volition earlier. "You have a business to run and family counting on you. That's a full plate for anyone."

Sensing she was gun-shy of probing the real reason, Jake shifted for a better view of her face. Failing to find the answer there, he stretched his arm across the back of the seat. "So you forgive me?"

"Fresh page," she agreed.

It felt so good to be trading smiles again, Jake gave her earlobe a gentle tug. "I've missed you," he said, going out on a limb.

"Me, too," she admitted, heat rising.

Jake moved his arm from the seat to rest lightly across her shoulder and cupped her upper arm with his hand. Her skin was like satin against his scuffed palm. He willed her to tip her face to his and draw closer. But he left the choice to her.

That small courtesy cradled Shelby in the eye of the storm. She lifted her gaze to his. His eyes reflected sky-shine from lightning strobes now tearing the heavens. But their depths were tropical waters, warm and inviting. Her nerves climbed on tiptoes as with his free hand, he traced her ear. His fingertips strew gooseflesh, stroking a path from the curve of her jaw to her chin.

Sudden thunder crashed so loudly, they both jumped. The lights in a tall sign that spelled out the mission name went out and came back on. Shelby arched her neck toward the passenger door, looking through the window and up at the flickering sign. "Got your Men Working sign?"

"Gonna be that tough, just getting a kiss?" Jake rumbled.

She phrased a blushing protest. He drew her face to his and smothered her words with a chuckle still on his lips.

The kiss was tenderly given, both a foretaste and memory stirrer. It transported Shelby back to Gram

Kate's kitchen and fierce kisses that had escalated into a heart storm she had been these past weeks sorting through to no definitive conclusion. And here she was in his arms, his lips plying sweetness, coaxing her to hit the Restart button and play it again Shelby.

There was power in the pause. She used it wisely and opened her eyes. Her hands were between them now, resting lightly on his chest. The tension in her fingers transmitted an unspoken message.

Jake responded accordingly, and let her go. The rain showed no sign of letting up. "Come on," he said, and reached for a summer-weight jacket folded on the seat. "Let's run for it."

Shelby scooted off the seat and out the door after him. Jake held the jacket aloft. She stepped off the running board and ducked beneath it with him. To little avail. The wind laughed at the jacket. They dashed across the lot, jumping shallow puddles. Gusty rain hammered the parking lot and lashed at them as they ran.

Jake held the door. Shelby ducked inside. Her dress was soaked. Her feet slid downhill in her platform sandals, and no mirror in sight. She plucked at her damp skirt and ran her fingers through wet curls.

Brady strode out of the adjoining kitchen. "I wasn't sure you'd come. Dinner won't be ready for an hour or so. I'm going to go tell my mom I'm back. You won't get tired of waiting dinner and leave, will you?" he asked, looking back.

"Of course not," Shelby said. "You go on and check in with your mother. We'll see if Cookie needs some help in the kitchen."

Chapter Fourteen

Cookie smiled at Shelby's introduction, shook Jake's hand in welcome, and gave them each hand towels. When they had dried off, Cookie pointed out a sink full of potatoes waiting to be scrubbed.

Shelby's wet dress had turned to clinging fabric. She tied a bibbed apron over it, and was washing her hands when who should stroll in but Monique Lockwood.

"Monique!" Cookie wheeled away from a stainless steel table that stood like an island in the middle of the kitchen. "I thought you had left us."

"I did," she replied, and fluffed her flaming red hair. "I'm filling in for my friend Patty. He's installing a secondhand computer in my apartment and it's taking him longer than he expected. So here I am. You have recruits, I see," she said, with a glance that encompassed both Shelby and Jake.

Cookie made first-name introductions.

"Come here often?" Monique quipped, with no sign of recognizing Shelby.

"First time for me," Jake said.

"You don't know what you've been missing. How about you?" she turned to Shelby.

"Not as much as I'd like," Shelby replied. Either Patrick had not pointed her out at the tearoom, or she hadn't made an impression.

"Monique is a writer," the cook said, beaming. "Her books will be in bookstores soon."

"I'd do a signing in your kitchen, Cookie. But who could afford it?" Seeing Jake and Shelby trade glances, Monique's grin widened. "Please don't take that disparagingly. This was home for me for a spell and a lifesaver. Then my friend Patty got me back on my feet."

Monique stepped up to the hand sink, and turned on the tap. "That's what I've taken to calling him, Cookie, 'my friend Patty.'"

"Patrick is one of our volunteers," explained the cook.

"Patrick Delaney. He's one of the city's leading attorneys," Monique said, punching the word *leading*. "I didn't know that though, until I ran into him at a lunch joint where it appeared I had been stood up. I assumed he remembered me from the mission and was being a nice guy when he invited me to join him. It was only after we'd ordered that he told me *he's* the lawyer I'd come to meet."

"Patrick's a big help around here, and an asset to our city," Cookie interjected.

"But not such a big shot, he forgets his friends," Monique said.

Shelby angled Jake another sidelong glance. He went on scrubbing spuds, taking no part in the conversation.

Not that Monique left any dead air for anyone else to insert a word edgewise. A loquacious woman in her midthirties, and oblivious to Shelby's identity, she launched into an account of her publishing experience from the acceptance of her book to the phone call in which she had asked for an early advance on royalties.

"You don't know what powerless is, until you're tapped out, no home and no one cares," she told them, sharing her feelings of helplessness at being turned down. "I'd worked harder on that book than I'd worked on anything in my whole life, and I never was any good at the wait-and-see game." Monique went on to relate her squeaky wheel retaliation—the bluff to sue.

"Looking back now, I see that the cover wasn't the problem. I was frustrated and angry and desperate. I kind of lost my grip and vented big time." She rolled repentant brown eyes and added, "Patty reasoned with me, friend to friend. He said that my conduct was unprofessional and a risk to my future as a writer."

"Precise and to the point. That's our Patrick," said the cook.

"Then he gave my hand a squeeze, as if to soften his words." Monique picked up a knife and used it to separate frozen hamburger patties. "He said if I would cease and desist with the cover tempest, he would do his best to persuade my editor to look at my next effort with an unbiased eye."

Shelby ducked her face over the sink, scrubbing the jacket right off a potato. Beside her, Jake broke his silence to ask Monique, "How's that going?"

"It's too soon to tell. I have the book outlined in

my head," she said. "But I've been waiting to settle into my new place before getting it down on paper."

Monique went on to say how much help she had received from Can-Do and from Patrick in easing back into the mainstream of life.

Cookie slapped oversize baking sheets down on the counter beside the box of frozen burgers Monique was hacking apart. "Not to change the subject, Monique, but you see the big brute coming across the dining room, there?"

Monique turned and looked through the open serving window, which separated the kitchen from the dining hall. "You mean Jig-Saw?"

"You're on a first-name basis, then?" Cookie asked. "He's been asking for your address."

"What'd you tell him?" countered Monique.

"I told him I didn't have it," Cookie said.

"Thanks, Cookie. I appreciate your concern," Monique told him. "Have you cleaned the milk cooler lately?"

"Be my guest," Cookie replied.

Shelby stepped away from the sink, making room for Monique who trotted off to the dining room with a sponge and a basin of soapy water.

"Shelby, if you'd put these patties on baking trays, I'll get the potatoes ready for the deep fryer," Cookie suggested.

Jake helped Cookie put the potatoes through a machine that turned them into fries. Alone at the stainless steel table, Shelby looked up from her appointed task to see the man Cookie had referred to as Jig-Saw limp to the milk cooler. The cooler was a few yards beyond the serving window, giving Shelby a bird's eye view. Jig-Saw was tall and starkly built, with short-clipped hair the color and texture of winter grass gracing a high, proud forehead. He had a strong nose and scar-engraved cheeks and taut jowls. The scars marred what might otherwise have been termed craggy and austere and handsome. His eyes were a piercing gray, intelligent, and deeply set with a wary expression Shelby mentally termed *pity-resistant*. All in all, he was embodiment of the walking wounded, both commanding and unforgettable. He rubbed his left hip, a look of pain dulling his expression as he and Monique talked.

Shelby couldn't hear their words over the noisy electric machine Jake and Cookie were using in the back kitchen. But by all appearances, Monique was at ease with the guy.

Cookie and Jake finished cutting the potatoes and retreated to a deep-fat fryer on the other side of the room. Monique was still working on the milk cooler, and chatting with Jig-Saw.

"Call it research for my next book," Shelby heard her respond.

"An exposé on your ex?" asked Jig-Saw.

"No, nothing so boring as that," Monique said. "It's about a lady and a lawyer who helps her believe she hasn't fallen so hard or so far that God can't give her a hand up."

"Any chance Patrick's turned you into an angel of mercy?" asked the man. "Because if he has, I could use a favor."

"What kind of a favor?"

"A place to stay. I wouldn't ask for myself, but my daughter is wanting to visit me," he said quickly.

"She doesn't know you're homeless?"

"No, and there's no reason to tell her. Provided

you'd cover for me" he added. "It would only be for a day."

"You'd want to make like it was your home, is that what you're saying?" asked Monique.

"If it's all right," he replied.

"Give me a little time to think about it." Monique swung to the serving window and slid her basin of water through it.

Quickly, Shelby averted her glance. "The patties are on the trays. What now?" she called to Cookie.

"Put them in the oven," he instructed, and adjusted the burner on the deep-fat fryer.

Jake had been processing information as well as potatoes. While Shelby hadn't mentioned that Patrick volunteered at the mission, it was reasonable by virtue of their past that they would have interests in common. Further, Monique's tearoom summary had confirmed that Jake's doubts of that day had been unfounded. What had gotten into him, anyway? He should have known Shelby wasn't one to manipulate with her own end in view, even if she did still hold feelings for Patrick. Which she very well might.

But then, he didn't back off from competition when bidding a job. Why would he, where someone as important as Shelby was, was concerned? He crowded out the practical considerations his mind had been repeating by rote all month and strolled over to transfer the trays of burgers to a convection oven and set about testing the waters.

"So what do you think?" he asked, as they slid the last tray into place.

"If it were up to me, I'd grill them," Shelby offered.

"I meant Monique," Jake returned, watching her. "I gather you two never met face-to-face."

"Just that glimpse at the tearoom." Shelby wiped her hands on her apron. "Apparently, she didn't notice us."

"Seems that way," Jake agreed. "So what are the odds on her getting a second chance at Parnell?"

"If it's up to me, she will."

"That's what I figured," Jake said. "You're a good sport, you know it?"

"Not really. I was livid for weeks."

"Change of heart?"

"Hearts will do that," she said and smiled so warmly, Jake allowed himself the liberty of reading into her words.

"It's going to be a little awkward, though, the day we do come face-to-face and she realizes who I am," Shelby continued.

"She'll thank you later for giving her a good story to tell," Jake predicted. "Better yet, she can sell it to your publisher, and you'll all live happily ever after."

"A how-to on how on to live happily ever after," she said with an oblique glance that made him grin. "Sounds like a bestseller to me."

Together, they prepared buns for the burgers, then put out the condiments. By the time the oven buzzer rang, a line had formed at the serving window and wrapped its way around the room.

Brady waited to eat with Jake and Shelby. His mother, Shelby noticed, had nervous hands and a weary, defeated demeanor. She explained that she and Brady had been en route to her brother's home in Iowa when their car broke down. The car held all their earthly treasures, things she was unwilling to leave behind. Her brother had been a week now, making arrangements to come collect them and their meager possessions.

"Go rest, if you want to," Brady told his mother, when she complained of feeling weary. "I'll stay with Jake a while, okay?"

His mother granted permission. Brady led Shelby and Jake to the lounge and brought out a board game. The board was a geography map of the old west. Each player got a share of play loot, a game piece and a handful of cards. There was a feather, too, symbolic of a writing quill. Each time a treaty was made, participating players were to touch the feather.

Shelby slipped off her damp shoes. Noticing, Jake reached down and tickled her toes with the feather. Brady followed suit, and chortled with boyish glee when Shelby squealed.

"Quit, now, or I'll confiscate your feather," she threatened with mock sternness.

Brady giggled and resumed mischievous efforts to tickle her feet.

"Hold it down, would you please?" a deep voice called across the room. "I'm talking long distance."

Shelby, Jake and Brady all swung around to the see the man with the scarred face at the pay phone.

"We're sorry," Shelby said, and touched her finger to her lips.

"Jig-Saw." Brady's voice dropped to a hush as he shrank into his chair.

Jake, who had been sitting with his back to the man, took a second gander and scratched his head. "The name doesn't ring a bell. But there's something familiar about the guy."

"It's not a common face. Poor man," murmured Shelby.

"It isn't his face, it's his voice." Jake's brow pleated. "Can't quite place it, though."

Shelby watched out of the corner of her eye as the man hung up the phone. "He looks lonely. Why don't you ask him if he'd like to join us, Brady?"

Brady hesitated, his expression uncertain.

"Sit tight, son. I'll ask." Jake shifted to his feet, and angled across the room.

Jig-Saw looked up from folding a slip of paper into his pocket. Recognition flashed in those ash-colored eyes, confirming Jake's suspicion that he should know him.

"Have we met?" Jake asked.

The man drew his hand across his face and wheeled away before Jake could thrust out his hand. Jake watched him limp away. But it wasn't the limp, it was those odd-colored eyes that fell into place. *Colton!* It struck Jake like a fully loaded eighteen wheeler.

"What was that all about?" Shelby murmured, looking from Jake to the door that had shut after Colton.

Even now, Jake's certainty was fading. Why would an icon in the advertising world be getting his meals at a homeless mission? Doubt crowding in, Jake kept his private thoughts private, and said, "Guess he doesn't want to join us. Let's finish our game, shall we?"

Shelby wasn't swallowing Jake's easy dismissal of Jig-Saw's brush-off. Something about the man was nagging at him. She could see it working on him. His sudden inattentiveness gave it away, too. His gaze kept returning to the door through which Jig-Saw had disappeared.

Chapter Fifteen

Jake and Shelby played several games with Brady before his mother came to collect him. Before leaving the mission, Jake excused himself for a word alone with the mission director. Shelby ducked into the ladies' room and tamed unruly curls. Jake and Mr. Weaver had emerged from the director's office by the time she reached the foyer.

"Tell Brady and his mom it's to help them get a fresh start in Iowa. No need in saying who," he added, shaking hands with Mr. Weaver.

"I'd like to keep in touch." Shelby retrieved a pad and pencil from her pocketbook and took down Brady's uncle's address in Iowa.

"He'll appreciate hearing from you both," Mr. Weaver said.

Shelby entrusted to Mr. Weaver a contribution toward Brady and his mother's travel expenses. He promised to pass it along, and bid them good evening.

Jake held the door for Shelby. She preceded him

out beneath clearing skies and asked on caught
breath, "What did Mr. Weaver say concerning Jig-
Saw?"

Jake was still reeling from the shock of recognizing Colt and the realization of how far and how fast
a man could fall. Uncertain how to tell her except
straight out, he stopped in the middle of the parking
lot.

"What is it?" Shelby asked, reaching for his hand.

"Colton." Jake pointed to the high-rise sign
across the way.

Shelby glanced at The Voyager paddling his canoe
along the infamous billboard and darted after Jake.
Confused, she said, "What about it?"

"That was him. Jig-Saw."

"*That* Colton? The Voyager? Joy's *father?* You
don't mean it!" she gasped.

"Afraid so." Jake reseated his cap. "As far as Mr.
Weaver knows, Jig-Saw is just another hard-luck
story. He had a bad accident some time ago and no
place to go when he was released from the hospital."

"But how does a guy pulling down that kind of
money end up in a homeless shelter?" cried Shelby.

"I don't know, and I don't like the scenarios that
leap to mind." Jake waited for her while she
searched her purse for her car keys. "Makes me all
the more uneasy about Joy. Funny he'd have a computer, but no home."

"He's planning on Joy coming to see him. I overheard him say so to Monique as she was cleaning
the milk cooler."

Jake listened intently as Shelby related to the best
of her ability the part of the conversation that she
had heard.

"Paula isn't going to agree to that," he said with certainty

"But he *is* Joy's father," said Shelby.

"And for that, he deserves consideration?" he countered.

"I have no idea. You're the one who has been there for them, I know that," Shelby said quickly.

"I'm sorry, I didn't mean to bark at you. I'm still having trouble believing it was him. And yet, I know it was." Jake unlocked her car door, and swung it wide, saying, "Let's just forget it for now, all right?"

Shelby tried not to feel hurt by the barrier he had dropped. It was obvious his encounter with Joy's father had him kicking the ends out of coffins on long-buried feelings. She wished, as she slid behind the wheel, that she had a deeper history with him, the kind that would have equipped her to be of some help.

True to his intention of shelving the whole business, Jake reminded her of the blues festival unfolding at Grant Park.

"It was just a thought, Jake. We don't have to go if you're not in the mood," Shelby said quietly.

"I don't know what to make of the information is all," he said touching once more on Colton.

"Stunned?" she said, with a sympathetic brush of hands.

"Something like that," he admitted, and squeezed her hand, finding healing in her touch. "I'll run my truck back to the motel lot where it'll be secure. Take me a few minutes to shower and change."

"You want me to pick you up there?" Shelby asked.

"We'd have to find a place to park. That'll be a real headache. How about I grab a cab and pick you up. How much time do you need?"

Wrinkles had dried into Shelby's dress. Her shoes were still damp. A soak to ease muscles growing stiff from too many bumps in the bumper car would do no harm, either. Measuring how much daylight remained of the long summer evening, she gave Jake her address and promised to be ready in forty minutes.

The fragrant soak was a short one. Shelby dried and styled her hair, and donned an ankle-length crinkle-pleated skirt. She buttoned and tucked in a crisp cotton blouse with a scooped neckline and loose sleeves that billowed to her elbows. Rolling the long edge of a paisley shawl, she tied it at her waist and turned the knot to the back. The gaily fringed swatch of linen accessorized the skirt nicely, as did hoop earrings and an antique locket. With two minutes to spare, Shelby spritzed her throat with juniper breeze body splash, slipped into her favorite platform sandals, and was waiting when Jake arrived.

He was clad in khakis and a blue shirt that drew Shelby's attention to his eyes the moment he swung open the cab door.

"Want a lift, pretty lady?" he said, and let go a whistle.

Pulse quickening at the open admiration in his eyes, Shelby laughed and countered, "My mama said don't take rides with strangers."

"Then climb on in here and we'll get better acquainted," he quipped, and tucked her in beside him. "Grant Park," he told the cabby.

The sun was setting as they climbed out of the cab

just a block from the heart of the festivities. There was a noisy glazed-eye quality about a city that Jake usually found wearing at the end of a day. But tonight, surrounded by music and the cacophony of voices, the cloud threatening the evening wasn't so much the wall of humanity closing in as concern over people Jake loved standing in hurt's way. He warred it stubbornly with a glib tongue and fluent flirtation that fooled Shelby not in the least. Rather it evoked in her both tenderness and a willingness to let the little actress out of the box if it gave him reprieve from the impending abrasions closing in on his family. So when he compared her skirt to peacock plumage, she spread it like a tail fan and curtsied just to make him smile. They wandered hand in hand until they found a patch of real estate large enough to settle.

"The ground's a little damp," Jake said, testing it. "We should have brought a blanket."

"Fret not," Shelby told him. She untied her shawl from her waist and spread it on the ground.

Jake awarded her ingenuity with an approving grin. "Always prepared. The hallmark of a true scout."

"Peacock troop, reporting for duty," Shelby replied, playing along, and laughed when he saluted.

Jake sat on the shawl beside her, ankles crossed, and waited until she had tucked her feet beneath the folds of her flowing skirt to stretch out on his back and rest his head in her lap.

"Make yourself comfortable," she drawled.

Unscathed by the tongue-in-cheek tip of her mouth, Jake distracted her with the music, urging, "Listen. Tugs at your eyelids, doesn't it?"

"If you say so," she acquiesced on a dry note, and pushed his cap brim down over his face. "Sweet dreams, Sign Man."

Jake grinned and hooked his cap over one knee, and found her face in the dusky twilight. The sky was beyond reach, the stars still in hiding. But a light shone from her eyes that he had not seen before. There were hidden depths there that bespoke endurance. The kind that provided a center, a hearth, a home fire, a buffer against wedges that sought to prevail. The peace that transcended understanding exposed his noisy front for what it was, and quieted him. Oblivious to the sea of humanity surrounding them, he savored the sensation of her hand light on his chest, keeping the beat of the music. He closed his eyes and didn't open them again until the dampness of the rain-soaked ground seeped through their cloth island. He felt her shiver.

"Cold?" he asked.

"Not bad." She crossed her arms, chafing them with her small hands.

Jake sat up and offered himself as a resting post. Shelby turned her knees to one side, and settled back against his chest. As an afterthought, she spread a swatch of skirt over his lap.

Jake smiled at her notion that the flimsy bit of crinkled pleats offered warmth.

"Sing," she said, as his arms closed around her.

"She can bake a cherry pie, fast as a cat can wink its eye," Jake sang, making music in her ear.

She curved her white neck, looking up at him. "Feeling better, Billy Boy?"

Acres of care fell away at that tender glance.

"Starting to," he said, and tucked a curl behind her ear. "You going to take me to church tomorrow?"

"You're staying then? I thought you might have changed your mind."

Because of Colton. She didn't say it. But he knew what she meant. "I'd just have to turn around and come back Monday morning," he reasoned.

"How flattering," she said. "There for a moment, I hoped my company had a little something to do with it."

"More than a little," he admitted and kissed her arching neck.

"Jake?" she began, emboldened by his closeness and the heat he was spreading with his kisses.

"Hmm?"

"I can't get Colton off my mind," she admitted as he rested his chin in her hair. "May I ask—was it because of the accident that Paula divorced him?"

"She didn't," Jake said.

Shelby turned in his arms to meet his eyes. "They're still married?"

"Technically, yes."

"But she hasn't seen or heard from him in all these years?"

"No," Jake replied, stroking the back of her hand with his thumb. "Why? What's on your mind?"

"It's none of my business, but I'm just trying to understand why Paula never told Colton about Joy."

In looking back, it was difficult for Jake to say at what point Paula made that decision. "She was pretty devastated by the accident. We all were, of course. But Paula even more so, partly because of her strong-willed battle to marry Colt in the first place," Jake said, remembering out loud.

Reaching back over the years, he recalled Paula, fresh out of high school, quarreling for parental blessing on her decision to forego college and marry Colt. The arguments had grown pretty heated, his parents deeply concerned that Paula was too young, too inexperienced and too in love to make a clear-headed decision. Jake shared as much with Shelby, concluding, "Once they were married, Mom and Dad accepted it. But it was awfully hard on Paula when the three people she loved most in the world collided on that dark two-lane road."

"She wasn't in the car with Colt?"

"No. He had just dropped her off to visit Gram."

"And still, she was a casualty," murmured Shelby, deeply saddened. Thinking of Colton, so scarred and broken, she asked, "How upset is Paula going to be to realize that Colt isn't all that he seems?"

"She found that out years ago," Jake replied in an emotionless voice that made Shelby wince.

Shifting in his arms, she asked softly, "What about you? Do *you* blame Colt for your parents' death?"

"No," Jake said. "I blame him for not being there to hold Paula when she cried."

Shelby's eyes drew tears at his tender-tough reply. It told her far more than she had asked, about Paula and Colton, and about Jake, too. He would never forsake her that way. The thought startled her, for it revealed the depth of her feelings for him. Quite unseen, he had been sinking roots into her heart all these weeks, even in separation. Marveling over it, she mused, "You're a pretty special guy, Jake."

"Could I get that in print?" he said.

Smiling, she reached up and patted his cheek. He hadn't shaved since morning. Razor stubble chafed her skin as he kissed her throat. His lips soothed what his skin had roughed. Shooting stars spiraled like pinwheels, showering sparks to far reaches. Shelby lifted her shoulder. He kissed that barrier, too, and kept on kissing her. The flame burned higher until finally, she created some breathing room.

He sighed knowingly, and asked her about her book.

"It's sweet of you to ask. But let's not go there," she said.

Jake contented himself holding her hand until the festival broke up at midnight. They practiced good-night kisses on the ride back to her building, and in the elevator ride up to her apartment, and had them perfected by the time they reached her door.

"The meter's running," she reminded, as Jake lingered.

"That what you call it?" Jake kissed her throbbing temple.

"The *cab* meter."

"Oh, that," he said, and silenced her soft laughter with another kiss. "I'll call you, okay?"

"Where have I heard those words?" she teased.

"I promise," he said, and kissed her one last time.

Shelby hadn't long to wait. Jake called her from his motel room as soon as he returned, just to say good-night.

"Did you call Paula?" she asked.

"No," he said. "It's late. It'd only keep her up, worrying."

Shelby heard the weariness in his voice, and asked

no more questions. I love you, Jake, she thought, and wished for the opening to say it out loud.

The next morning, Shelby took Jake to her parents' home church only to learn her folks were out of town. Afterward, they lunched at a neighborhood restaurant, then strolled Navy Pier, soaking up sun on the boardwalk and watching people wandering in and out of the shops. They bought seed from a vending machine and fed the gulls, then caught a water taxi to Shedd Aquarium. It was one of Shelby's favorite places. She enjoyed sharing it with Jake. He didn't mention Colton all day. Respecting his bid to avoid the subject, she didn't bring it up, either.

Jake bought posies from a corner cart on the way to the restaurant they had chosen for dinner. Excellent food, fresh flowers, candlelight and music made for a lovely intimate dinner. Afterward, at Jake's invitation, Shelby stepped out onto the dance floor and into his arms.

Jake drew her closer. They danced out the slow number and another that followed before he broke the comfortable silence and mentioned her book.

"What book?" she bid for another subject.

He said, "Forget it, then, if you don't want to talk about it. It's not getting me anywhere, asking."

"Where is it you want to be?"

"Right here's nice," he said, and cradled her cheek with the hollow of his hand.

"For me, too."

"God was surely smiling when I bumped into you yesterday."

"Yesterday? Let's see." She fit a finger to a dimpled cheek and sucked her bottom lip, thinking.

"Would that be the day you said I needed a better man?"

He chuckled and admitted, "That was before I knew that Patrick walks on water."

"Kind of stunned me, too," Shelby said, her playfulness receding. "He hasn't always. At first I dragged him to the mission kicking and screaming. He had to have changed right before my eyes. But I didn't see it. I was too busy."

"With your job?"

"And my writing."

"Regrets?" he asked softly.

"About Patrick? No," she said without hesitation. "I admire him for his goodness. But I've moved on."

Jake held her close and didn't ask if she loved Patrick. She didn't. Not with the love from which lovers were carved. She saw that clearly from Jake's embrace. Wanting him to know it, too, so that they could be finished with this conversation forever, she said, "Patrick told me when he broke it off that he needed someone who loved him enough to put everything into the marriage, and not hold anything back."

"Including your writing?"

She nodded. "I guess he saw I was afraid of losing it, and my identity, too. He took exception, saying there was no fear in love. He was right, of course. I see that now."

"New glasses?" Jake asked with a tender smile.

She laced her fingers with his as they danced, kissed the back of his hand and murmured, "No. A new man."

A wild relief swept over him. He pocketed her into

deep shadows, whispering her name and endearments
between soft kisses. She slipped her arms around his
waist, tunneling between shirt and jacket. The kiss
deepened, expelling forever the ghosts of kisses past.

Later, when Jake saw her home, Shelby didn't invite him to linger. Aloud, she reasoned that they both
had to work in a few hours. Jake intended to finish
the last dry cleaning store by noon tomorrow. Then
he would go home. She wouldn't see him again until
Gram Kate's birthday party the following Saturday.

Shelby dreaded the separation. At the same time,
the stardust needed a chance to settle. Nothing in her
past had prepared her for love that came out of broken dreams and all but consumed her. Yet there it
was, pure light, radiating hope and inexpressible joy
with her every thought of him.

Jake met Shelby for breakfast the next morning.
They wouldn't be able to say their goodbyes later,
as Shelby had a lunch meeting, and a crowded afternoon. So they lingered long over coffee gone cold,
went over their plans for the following weekend and
added to the heat of the morning with one last embrace before going their separate ways.

Then Jake finished his job, and left the city behind,
already counting the days until they would be together again.

Chapter Sixteen

Paula and Joy had stayed at the house and looked after Gram while Jake was gone. They were eating dinner when he walked in.

Gram Kate beamed and stretched out her hands to him. "Jake! How nice of you to drop by. Have a bite with us, won't you?"

"Did you finish the job?" asked Paula.

"Wrapped it up a little after lunch," he said. "What's this—new potatoes?"

"Fresh out of the garden. The green beans, too," Paula said. "Joy picked them."

"Good for you, sport. Did you keep the weeds pulled, too?" Jake asked from the sink.

"Uh-huh. You owe me big time." Joy had her back to him and her finger in a magazine. She swung around in her chair. "Did you see Shelby while you were in Chicago?"

"Yes. She's coming Saturday for the birthday party," he said.

"Is it your birthday, dear?" Gram Kate spoke up. "Remind me to bake a ca-ca—"

"It's *your* birthday, not his," Joy interjected.

"Saturday, Gram. The whole town is coming," Paula said.

"Aunt Wendy must be right about you, Uncle Jake. She said you had it bad," Joy drawled, arching Jake a glance.

Jake draped the damp hand towel over her shoulder and tugged her braid in passing.

Joy turned calculating eyes from her open magazine, where her father was featured in a full-page ad, to Jake and asked, "Are you going to marry her and move to Chicago?"

"Chicago?" Jake echoed.

"Sure. That's were Shelby works, isn't it? I'm looking on the bright side—if you move to Chicago, it'd give me a chance to know Dad," Joy explained, "which I could anyway, if Mom would quit treating me like a baby. I'm old enough make up mind about him, don't you think, Uncle Jake?"

Jake dodged the question, asking, "So what do I owe you for weeding my garden?"

Joy darted her mother a defiant glance. "Buy me a bus ticket and we'll call it even."

"Don't be ridiculous, you're not going anywhere," Paula snapped. "Sit up straight, would you please? And put that magazine down while you eat."

"I'm finished," Joy said. She bolted from her chair, magazine in hand, flounced out through the porch and slammed the screen door behind her.

"She's going to break hearts someday," Gram Kate mused.

"Sounds to me like it's her mother's will she's set

on breaking," Jake observed. He squeezed Paula's shoulder in passing and added, "But hang tough, you're still the boss, sis."

"So why am I finding it so hard to follow my intuition and flat out refuse to even consider letting her see him?" Paula muttered, rubbing her temples.

"Because you're afraid you'll ignite a fight you can't win," Jake said, as gently as he knew how. "The good news is, you're worrying needlessly. Colt doesn't have the wherewithal to fight."

Paula spared him a dry glance and replied, "No more than you're average kazillionaire."

"Less. A good deal less. Seriously," said Jake.

"What are you saying?"

"I bumped into Colton while I was in Chicago," Jake told her. "At a homeless shelter."

"A homeless shelter?" Paula's hand flew to her throat.

Gram jumped out of her chair. "How much do they need? Where's the cookie jar? I'll send them some muh—muh—matches."

"Hush, Gram, I can't think." Paula's voice, sharp with shock, fell in contrition. "I'm sorry, Gram. I'm sorry." She circled the table and hugged Gram's neck.

"There, there, dear. I lose things, too." Gram patted Paula's hand absently. She left the table, taking the salt and pepper shakers to the sink and her empty plate to the living room.

Jake saw Paula's face contort at the strain of converging anguish. He shifted her empty chair out from the table in wordless invitation. She circled back to it, but didn't sit down. "I can't believe it. Are you sure it was him, Jake?"

"No mistake about it, it was Colton, all right," Jake said.

"You spoke to him?"

"He didn't give me the chance. He didn't want to be recognized."

"Well of course you'd recognize him," said Paula, frowning. "Half the planet knows that face."

"Not anymore. He's been in an accident. He's pretty scarred up," Jake told her.

Paula's color fled. She felt behind her for her chair, dropped and sat emotionless as he repeated what had transpired.

"Colton always did spend freely." Paula marshaled table crumbs with a trembling hand. "Joy is my life," she said, tears rising. "I can't entrust her to him when I don't even know if he's capable of basic parenting."

"Tell him so."

Paula shuddered and dropped her face in her hands, wiping away tears. "I don't owe him a reason. I'll just say no. Let him read whatever he wants into it."

Jake had no quarrel with that. The accident that had occurred all those years ago was just that—an accident. As he had told Shelby, he didn't blame him for the tragic consequences. However, Colt was responsible for the careless choices he had since made, and the far-reaching consequences touching Joy and Paula still today.

After dinner, Jake closed himself in his office. He wished the work week was gone and Shelby was here with him. Her presence was a buffer between him and the uncertainty of this business with Colton. Her touch and the light in her eyes covered his doubts about her ex-fiancé, his own crowded life and the isolating miles. Needing to hear her voice, Jake picked up the phone and dialed.

Shelby had had a full day and was late arriving home. The phone was ringing when she walked in.

"Miss you." Jake's voice warmed her ear.

"Me, too," she said. "How was your drive home?"

"Uneventful. Got a little rough at dinner, though," he said, and told her about it.

"What'd Joy say when you related her father's circumstances?" Shelby asked.

"She had left the table by then. Paula said if Colt wants Joy to know his circumstances, he'll tell her himself."

Shelby sympathized with Paula's difficult position before the conversation moved ahead.

"I phoned the mission this afternoon. Brady's uncle arrived yesterday. They left for Iowa this morning," she said by and by. "I was working on a card when you called. There's room for a line from you if you like," she said, after sharing what she had written.

Jake sent along his greetings, then promised to call again.

They spoke each night that followed. Jake was watching the weather with Gram's birthday party in view when Shelby phoned him on Thursday.

"The girls have a garden party in mind. Hope it doesn't rain," he told her. "You might want to bring—"

"My sunflower dress?" she interjected.

"You're pretty sunny in that. May hold back the

rain," he agreed, and chuckled. "But I was thinking more along the lines of that dress you dropped by the cleaners."

"A little formal, wouldn't you say?"

"Depends on how you look at it," countered Jake, emboldened by the smile in her voice. "Of course you'd have to get here tomorrow afternoon before the courthouse closes so we can get a marriage license."

"Very cute, Jake."

"So you're sticking to Plan E then?"

"E?" she echoed.

"Elopement."

"I did say that, didn't I?"

"In your own bittersweet words."

Smiling, Shelby twined the phone cord around her finger, cautioning, "Keep it up, and I may call your bluff."

"It's no bluff," he said. "I've got the preacher's number jotted down right here. 1-555-1212."

"That's directory assistance, Jake."

"I could use some assistance." He made the most of his joke. "Hello, Operator? Something wrong here. I've been put on hold."

Shelby sensed serious intent beneath Jake's levity. *There is no fear in love.* In his arms, that was so. But the miles separating them left a crack through which slipped the issue that had come between her and Patrick. She shied from thinking history could repeat itself. Jake would never forsake the woman he loved. Knowing it as surely as she knew anything, Shelby said, "You're so very patient. That's what I love about you, Jake."

"Love?" he echoed.

"Is that what you heard? Must have slipped," she said, and laughed softly. "I'll see you Saturday, Billy Boy."

Encouraged at how well she'd nibbled his test bait, Jake went out to the shop and made preparations for a sign. He had made a lot of signs over the years. But his heart was in this one. He ran a pattern off on his computer, spread it on Paula's workbench and spread a piece of screen wire over it. Then he heated clear glass tubes and bent them into shape to match the pattern.

The next day Jake found a discarded neon window sign in the boneyard at the Bloomington shop. The frame and transformers would work for his new sign. He stripped away the glass spelling out the café's name and the words *Open* and *Closed* and took the frame home with him. After dinner, Jake mounted the new glass, attached three transformers and wired the transformer leads to the glass electrodes.

Joy came sidling into the neon workshop as he was testing out the sign.

"What's that for?" she asked as the message, *Marry Me?* lit up.

"What do you think?" he replied.

She rolled her eyes and dismissed the sign with a sniff. "I got a blue ribbon on my cake at the fair last week," she told him.

"Then all that practice paid off. Well done," Jake said.

"Dirk asked me to ride the rides. But I wouldn't, 'cause I caught him on the Ferris wheel with this orange-haired twerp who belongs to his 4-H club."

"Plenty of time and plenty of Dirks out there," Jake soothed.

"Who cares? He's a know-nothing turkey, anyway. He acts like Dad's a sissy or something. Because of the billboard, I mean. Like modeling is just for girls. But I say Dad's free to make a living however he wants, don't you think?"

"It's his choice, his life," Jake said. "It's no different with you and me, blondie. Every day we make choices we have to live by."

"You, maybe. But Mom makes all of mine," she complained.

"She's just trying to teach how to choose for yourself."

"What's wrong with wanting to see Dad?"

"That's not my call," Jake replied, getting out of the middle.

"You always say that," Joy complained. "Makes me want to scream."

"I'll try to remember that, when I have kids of my own."

Met with a cold stare, Jake's grin felt out of place. He tried to redirect Joy's attention to the choices spelled out in neon. "Pull a chain," he prompted.

Joy chose without hesitation and smirked as the word *No* lit up.

"You can sweep up for me, if you want." Jake overlooked her petulance.

"Better not. Wouldn't want to get in your way," she said, and let the door slam on her way out.

Jake cleaned up the shop, took the sign inside and went to bed, debating presentation. With extended family and a good part of Liberty Flats coming for

Gram's birthday, it was going to be a job, finding the right time and place.

The answer came in the night. The next morning, Jake strung a cord through the attic to the catwalk atop the house, and plugged in the neon sign. He pulled the chain, testing the only answer he wanted to hear.

Neon flashed affirmatively to the vivid red question, Marry Me? Satisfied, Jake went downstairs and made coffee. Gram was still in bed, so he took his cup back up on the catwalk. Eager as a kid awaiting Christmas morning, he watched the street until he ran out of coffee and returned to the kitchen.

Gram was puttering around in her housecoat, sifting through drawers. When Jake questioned her, she couldn't remember what she was looking for.

He settled her at the table with coffee and cream, and had breakfast on the table by the time Shelby arrived. Pink suit, short skirt, white tights hugging slim shapely legs. Curls shining and her face alight, too. Jake registered this and much more in the heartbeat it took him to unhook the screen.

"Hi. I got an early start," she said, a little piece of heaven walking into his arms, with cloud-soft hair and skin and full moist lips smiling at him. "Did you save me any coffee?"

"We'll get to that," Jake said. He kissed her and would have taken her up to the catwalk then and there except Gram was on her feet, trying to put the electric pot on the burner.

Shelby slipped out of Jake's embrace and renewed acquaintance with Gram Kate. Gram Kate mistook her for Paula, and then Wendy. After breakfast, Gram told her, "I'll wash the dishes, Jill. You're going to miss your ride. Here they are now."

It was Paula, letting herself in. Joy scuffed along at her heels. Dressed in a black T-shirt, black jeans and a demeanor to match, she brushed past Shelby without speaking.

"Joy?" prompted Paula. "Aren't you going to say hello?"

"Hi," Joy muttered with a half-hearted wave. "Where's the Christmas lights, Uncle Jake? I'm going to string the white twinkly ones over the rose arbor. Help me, okay?"

"In a little while," Jake promised. "I hear a car."

Joy sauntered to the window. "Uncle Hershel and Aunt Marge," she said, with a spark of animation. "Uncle Hershel brought his fiddle."

"Gram's sister and her husband," Jake told Shelby. "Marge brings three-bean salad to all the family shindigs, and Hershel brings music."

"Oh, dear. I didn't...did you? Change the sheets in the guest room, would you, Wendy?" Gram said to Shelby.

"I changed them yesterday, Gram," Paula said. She winged Shelby a quick glance. "You don't mind staying at my house, do you?"

"Whatever is convenient," Shelby replied.

"You can have my room, I'll sack out here on the sofa," Joy offered. "Uncle Jake doesn't care, do you Uncle Jake?"

"Suit yourself," Jake said. He caught Shelby's hand in his. "Come along and I'll introduce you."

Uncle Hershel was a portly, red-faced, amiable man. He beamed at Shelby. "Pleased to meet you."

"You must be the little author. How nice to make

your acquaintance, dear." A thin, thistle-haired woman with Gram Kate's eyes, and a covered dish in hand, Marge smiled brightly. "Three-bean salad. The dish is a little drippy, it has been in the ice chest."

"Why don't I get your luggage?" Jake offered.

"While I poke this in the fridge," Marge agreed, nodding. "Come along, Hershel and we'll jog Kate's memory." She strode up the path to the house arm in arm with her husband.

Two more cars had pulled in as Shelby was trailing Jake with luggage. Within minutes, the whole place churned with Jacksons, their mates and their offspring. All of them were loaded down with food and presents and potted plants and plans to dress the yard in party garments.

The men rolled up their sleeves and drove stakes on the lawn to pitch a striped canopy in case of rain. The women had a penchant for organized chaos that delivered surprising results. Shortly before noon, Jake finished setting up chairs and tables beneath the canopy, and joined Shelby in the porch swing.

"It looks like a garden magazine centerfold." Shelby indicated with a sweep of her hand the transformation achieved by creative lighting and multiple seating arrangements, potted plants and a trickling fountain. "Your sisters should go into business."

Jake rubbed a smudge of flower pollen off her chin. "You did your share of arranging flowerpots."

She smiled. "Just stopping to smell the roses."

"The roses have seen more of you than I have," he complained, and pulled her to her feet. "Paula's got a ham in the oven she'd like someone to fetch. I think we can handle that, don't you?"

"Certainly," Shelby said. Enticed by the twinkle in his eye and his hand pressed to the small of her back, she led the way down the porch steps, all too eager for a moment alone with him.

Chapter Seventeen

Jake's Jeep was blocked by family vehicles. Shelby gave him her car keys. They drove across town to Paula's house. Jake took her suitcase from the trunk and led the way inside. Shelby took the ham out of the oven while Jake carried her luggage back to Joy's bedroom.

"What do you know. Dessert!" he called to her on his way back through the living room.

Shelby declined his offer to share the candy bar he had found in Joy's room. "I'm saving my appetite for Aunt Marge's three-bean salad," she claimed.

"I hate eating alone," Jake protested, and patted the sofa in invitation.

Shelby joined him there. At his coaxing, she shared the half-melted chocolate bar with him, and melted herself when he traced the gold chain on her neck. A shower of phantom sparks radiated from his touch.

"Any pictures inside?" He fingered the antique locket that hung in the hallow of her throat.

"I've been saving that for someone special," she said.

He brought his other hand to the locket, seeking the catch. The concentrated effort put lines in his brow and goose bumps on her skin. Her fingers brushed his as she opened the locket. He murmured at the absence of a picture inside, and was gathering her into his arms when the phone rang. It was Joy.

"Uncle Jake? Mom's waiting to slice the ham. What're you guys doing, anyway?"

"We're on our way." Jake hung up the phone, and sighed. "Duty calls. Shall we go?"

"I thought I'd freshen up first."

"You're fresh enough for me," he teased. "But give me a call, and I'll come pick you up when you're ready."

When Jake had gone, Shelby showered and shook the folds from her sunflower dress. She had shopped for a wide-brimmed hat just for the occasion. It was lavishly adorned with flowers and yellow ribbon, a perfect compliment to the dress.

As was Jake's tie, when he arrived, his shirt starched, his trousers crisply pleated and his shoes polished to a picture-glass shine.

"Did I mention sunflowers become you?" he said of her dress.

"This old thing?" She flashed a coy smile and fluttered her lashes.

"You're radiant. I mean it," he said, and kissed her cheek.

"And speaking of vivid…" Shelby laughed and trailed her fingers over the screen-painted greenery vining up the yellow tie. "Looks like something from *Jack and the Beanstalk.*"

"That's where impulse shopping will get you." He feigned injured feelings. "I can change it if you think it's too much."

"Don't you dare. A little smoothing is all that it needs."

"Smooching?" He pretended to misunderstand.

"Smoothing." She enunciated it clearly, and laughed. "I move the mutual admiration society adjourn for the birthday party before we succumb to our own devices. Do I hear a second?"

"I second the motion." Jake laughed and kissed the hands that straightened his tie. He folded one neatly over his arm and covered it with his hand. "Before they start without us."

They arrived to such a crowd, it was unlikely they would have been missed by anyone other than Joy. The house, the yard and the canvas canopy overflowed with guests, a token of the affection in which Gram Kate was held by both family and community.

The guests served themselves from the endless buffet spread in the kitchen. They ate their fill at tables and lawn chairs and garden benches scattered throughout the yard. Gram received such a mountain of presents, the grandchildren had to peel off the wrappings when her attention strayed from the task.

Afterward, Paula asked Shelby to help serve the cake and punch. They had prepared a beautiful table set beneath the striped canopy. A festoon of ribbons and paper flowers adorned the lacy tablecloth. Emmaline from Newt's Market had baked a huge sheet cake. The icing spelled out a birthday greeting in colors to match the rainbow sherbet that floated atop the punch.

"We'll serve the cake if you two want to man the punch bowl," Paula said to Shelby and Wendy.

"Here. You dip, I'll pass you the cups." Wendy gave Shelby the silver ladle and a crystal cup.

Joy crowded between Shelby and her mother, matches in hand. "I get to light the candles."

Gram beamed as Uncle Hershel brought out his violin. Friends and family closed in and sang the birthday song. When the last notes faded, Gram blew out the candles. But before they could be plucked from the cake, she picked up the abandoned matches and began relighting the candles.

"Gram! You blew them out once," reminded Joy.

Confused, Gram Kate paused with the lighted match in hand. "Hot, hot." She tried to shake it out, but dropped it instead into one of the paper flowers. The tissue paper went up in flames.

A collective gasp rose from the party goers. Jake bounded forward and eased Gram out of harm's way. Shelby, at ground zero, tossed a cup of punch on the flames. The ribbon connecting the garland of paper flowers smoldered. Intent on preventing the flames from spreading over the table Shelby grabbed another cup. She dipped and tossed and dipped and tossed until Joy screeched, "That's enough! It's out!"

Shelby blanched to see sherbet dripping off Gram Kate's dress. It was trickling down Jake's pant leg, too and the party garments of half a dozen guests.

Cheeks hot, Shelby hurried around the table and in a flurry of apologies, dabbed at Uncle Hershel's tie with her scented lace-trimmed hanky.

"Forget it! We'll wash." He brushed aside her concern as if flames and punch flew at all the Jackson parties.

Smothered snickers and giggles caught a draft that carried the sherbet-splattered guests along. Most chortled even as they sponged their clothes. Emmaline wrinkled her cute snub nose and promised Jake, "I'll send you my dry cleaning tab."

"You shouldn't have left the matches where she could get them," Paula scolded Joy.

"At least I didn't throw punch on everybody," Joy huffed.

Paula poked the matches into her apron pocket, and propelled Joy toward the house. "Run get a fresh tablecloth. Come on girls, let's clean up this mess. All's well that ends well."

Shelby wasn't sure it had. She caught her lip, watching as Joy stormed to the house like a bull with her head down.

At Shelby's side, Wendy soothed, "Pay no attention to Joy. She has her nose out of joint is all."

"What's wrong?" murmured Shelby.

Paula shot Wendy a warning glance. "Would you wash out the punch bowl and make some fresh punch, please, Wendy?"

"I apologize for Joy," Paula said, when Wendy had gone. "She's a little old to be reacting this way. But then, Jake is like a father to her."

"Reacting?" Shelby echoed. "To what?"

"You haven't been up to the catwalk yet?"

Shelby tipped her head back, and eyed the decorative wrought-iron railing atop the house. "I didn't realize it was accessible. Why? What's up there?"

"I'm sorry. I seem to have spoken out of turn." Paula's mouth tipped in an enigmatic smile.

Jake's sisters closed ranks and filled the air with chatter. Mystified by the whole lot of them, and feeling like the odd man out, Shelby lent her efforts to cleaning up the mess she had made of the table and gave up trying to understand Jacksons.

Jake put Joy in charge of helping Gram change her dress. He donned a fresh pair of trousers, and found Shelby at the punch bowl again. A line had formed. She was filling cups as fast as Wendy could hand them off.

He slipped up behind her and tugged at her hat. "Now you're getting the hang of it."

Shelby's color rose as she turned and angled him a brave smile.

"Mom says take Gram and Aunt Marge some cake and punch," Joy said as she proceeded to help herself from the serving side of the table. "You can come sit with us if you want, Uncle Jake."

"You go ahead, I'll wait for Shelby," Jake replied.

"I need help carrying the punch," entreated Joy, three plates of cake in hand.

Jake dropped something between a sigh and kiss on the nape of Shelby's neck, then followed Joy to the rose arbor where Gram and her sister were sitting. He distributed the cups of punch and chatted a moment before joining Uncle Hershel on the porch.

"Say, Jake, but doesn't that little gal of yours have a good arm on her?" greeted Uncle Hershel.

Jake grinned and flicked the spot on Hershel's tie. "Now to fine-tune her aim."

"Setting her sights on you, you mean?" Hershel cackled. "I kind of wondered myself if she knew the whole business."

"The business has never been better," Jake said.

"I'm not talking about the sign business, boy. I'm talking about Kate. She's slipped considerably in the past few months. "

Jake tried to change the subject. But Uncle Hershel, having none of it, set his plate and cup aside, and leaned forward, forearms resting on his knees. "You got a right to a life of your own, son. Kate'd be the first to tell you so if she was up to par."

"I appreciate your concern, Uncle Hershel, but—"

"Hear me out, son," Hershel wagged an open hand before Jake's face, forestalling interruption. "There's some mighty nice retirement apartments these days, some with assisted living. Marge and I have been looking into it ourselves. No point in holding out so long we become a burden to others, you see what I mean?"

"Gram Kate isn't a burden," Jake said.

Hershel patted him on the shoulder. "That's a nice sentiment, boy. But if you're serious about that pretty little gal, then you need to take her into consideration, too."

The endless commotion, playing host and holding his tongue in the face of well-intentioned advice ground away at Jake. He counted the hours until he could steal away with Shelby, light the question and settle the matter once and for all. "Can I get you some more punch, Uncle Hershel?" Jake offered. "Another piece of cake, maybe?"

"No thanks, Jake. I'm watching my figure. But you go ahead. And don't forget what I told you, now, you hear?"

Chapter Eighteen

Shelby eased back into her pinching shoes as Jake sidled up at the tail end of the refreshment line.

"Save any punch for me?"

The smile lighting his face was refreshment to Shelby. "That, and the biggest piece of cake I could find." She peeled back the napkin covering the plate she had set aside for him.

Jake grinned. "Well done. I heard a rumor there was an unoccupied patch of grass and a nice shade tree around front. Interested?"

"Very," she said, and took the arm he offered.

Jake strolled her past a cluster of children playing dodge ball on the front lawn. Joy turned from her companions, and tossed the ball.

"Think fast, Uncle Jake!"

Jake blocked it with his foot, passed Shelby the cups of punch, and flung the ball back into the circle of children. They giggled and scattered so as not to be tagged by the ball.

"Missed me!" chanted Joy.

Jake tugged her plaited braid in passing, and led the way to the widespread maple tree. A massive old tree, it was set apart from the house and front lawn by low shrubs and a brick path that widened into an inviting paved outdoor living space leading up to the front portico. The trunk of the tree served as a back rest and partially screened them from the children's game and wild tosses of the ball.

"I was thinking that after dinner we could go up on the catwalk and watch the sunset," Jake suggested.

Intrigued, Shelby tucked her feet beneath the fan of her skirt and asked, "What is it with the catwalk? Paula mentioned it too."

"She did, did she?" He tantalized her with a enigmatic grin and shared the double-size wedge of cake. "By the way, how are you at ladders?"

"That depends. Is it attached to one of your crane trucks?"

Jake chuckled. "I'm never going to live that down, am I?"

Shelby smiled and brushed crumbs from her lap. Jake reached for her hand. Together, they watched a boy pedal up the street on his bicycle. He pulled up on the handlebars, rode a wheelie for a half a block, then turned and paraded past again.

"Is that who I think it is?" asked Shelby.

"Dirk?" Jake grinned and nodded. "Word is he's sweet on a girl in his 4-H club."

"Perhaps he's having second thoughts," Shelby said.

"For all the good it will do him. Joy isn't much at second chances."

"I don't know about that. She wants to see Colton, doesn't she?" Shelby reasoned.

"That's different," Jake said. "She's curious, naturally."

Before Shelby could invite him to elaborate, the children's game ball splashed through the bird bath, bounced over the bricks and came rolling under the maple tree. Joy meandered over to retrieve it.

Jake changed the subject accordingly. "I've been thinking about your problem book this past week and the question comes to mind—who murdered Mr. Weedman?"

"You think he was murdered?"

"Are you saying he wasn't?"

Shelby settled her punch cup on the empty cake plate. "First, tell me who you find suspicious."

"Old man Blatchford, for starters. The body was found in his field."

"He's rather feeble as suspects go," Shelby said.

"Exactly! Frailty deflects suspicion." Thoughts engaged, Jake watched idly as Joy dried the ball in the grass and studiously ignored the bicycling boy wonder, who was making another pass up the street. "Then there's the tough guy on the bean crew—what's his name?"

"Dudley?"

"Right, Dudley. Had a row with Weedman, as I recall. Which could make him either a rogue, or a diamond in the rough."

"You've given this some thought, I see."

"But of course," Jake said. "If you have a problem, I have a problem."

"What a nice sentiment," Shelby murmured.

Taking that to mean she was open to advice, Jake

said, "If you're still stuck, you could write the last chapter and work backward. By the way, does Weedman have any life insurance? If so, his wife would make a good suspect."

"Write backward?" She dismissed the idea with a smile that broadened as she asked, "And how in the world can you suspect his wife? She hasn't even appeared on the page."

"That in itself is suspicious," Jake said. "I propose we collaborate."

"Why? Who do you have in mind for a villain?"

"I'll leave that up to you. But I'm more than willing to help you narrow down that love triangle thing."

Shelby wagged her head at his leading grin. "I should have seen that one coming."

"So now *I'm* on the suspect list?" Jake feigned injury.

"Jack's the hero, Uncle Jake. He couldn't have done it,"

Shelby looked to find Joy standing a few yards away with the ball tucked under her arm. "Who said anything about Jack?"

"Jake, Jack. What's the difference?" Joy said.

"Wait a second, wait a second!" objected Shelby, the conversation gone suddenly awry. "Joy, how did you know about Jack?"

Joy cut her eyes from Dirk, who was pedaling away, arms folded across his chest, to Jake. She blanched and darted away without answering.

"You told her?" Shelby leaned away from Jake, the better to see his face. Once, she had seen a stray pup get that same look as the dog catcher's net closed over him. "Jake?"

His jaw twitched. But he didn't affirm or deny it. Or try to stop her as she slipped into her shoes, and crossed the yard to where Joy was watching her cousins from the sidelines.

"Joy?" Shelby said quietly.

Joy pivoted. Her freckled cheeks turned pink. "Okay, so I snooped. Big deal."

Had she misread him, then? Confused, Shelby glanced from Joy to Jake, coming to join them.

"If you didn't want it read, you should have secured your file." Joy took the offensive. "A first-grader could have opened it."

"Joy! Are you saying that I think your saying?" Paula asked, overhearing from the nearby portico. "Did you read Shelby's story without her permission?"

"I was just curious," Joy whispered, her meek tone at odds with the mutiny flagging her cheeks, as her mother joined them.

"You did, then? Joy Blake, if it's not one thing, it's another. What am I going to do with you?" Paula huffed in exasperation.

"As it turns out, it's looking as if I won't finish it anyway, Paula," Shelby said quietly, hoping to relieve Paula's embarrassment and Joy's growing resentment against her.

"Thanks, Shelby. But Joy's conduct is the issue," Paula said.

"What about Uncle Jake? He read it, too. Didn't you, Uncle Jake?"

Shelby was about to explain that she had asked Jake to read her story. But the contrition in his blue eyes stopped her cold.

"Go on, tell her Uncle Jake!"

"That's enough, Joy," Paula rebuked, and pointed

Joy toward the house. She spoke to the remaining children. They scooped up their ball and with a collective backward glance, trotted around to the other side of the house.

Jake's gaze shifted from Shelby to Paula hurrying after Joy. He shoved his hands into his pockets and offered no defense. A moment ago, the air had writhed with words. Now it was so quiet, Shelby heard the breeze purring high in the trees. Eons passed as she waited for Jake to explain.

"Mad?" he asked finally.

"Then you did read it? Before I asked you to?" said Shelby, heart constricting.

He nodded.

"Why didn't you say so?"

Jake squinted out of one eye and rubbed the back of his neck. "I wanted to. But you were pretty upset over Mr. Wiseman at the time."

"And in the time since?" she asked.

"Didn't figure you'd find out," he admitted.

"Jake!"

"I'm just being honest."

"Now *that's* rich."

Jake reached to stop her from flight. Shelby stiffened her arm beneath his hand. "It was on the screen when I turned on the computer," he said and let his hand fall away. "I started reading before I realized what it was. I should have stopped, but I'd swallowed the hook, so to speak."

"I told you I had a problem with people reading my stuff before it was finished. I was very clear about that, Jake."

"I know."

"But you did it anyway?" She paused, waiting.

When he offered nothing, her hurt gave rise to frustration and anger. "Is it any wonder I haven't written anything worth reading since leaving this place?"

"Now wait a second," Jake objected. "You're surely not blaming that on me?"

"What if I am?" she said, and tilted her chin.

"Your writing wasn't going well when you arrived," he reminded.

"I soon found my stride."

"And without blaming Patrick. Imagine that."

Stung, she retorted, "Patrick never hacked into my work."

"And for that lack of interest, you commend him?"

"It wasn't a lack of interest, it was respect for what I do."

"Oh, that's right. I forgot. Impeccable Patrick."

"So now you're jealous?"

"Should I be?" he countered, then looked past her, distracted by approaching guests.

Shelby turned as Emmaline, the cake baker, strolled across the grass between her uncle and Liberty Flat's mayor. Jake cupped his ear to some smiling remark Emmaline was calling to him. To Shelby he said, "Could we finish this later?"

It wasn't a question. The party was breaking up. He strode to meet his approaching guests, and with a rejoinder for Emmaline, resumed his role as host. Shelby left him to his goodbying, climbed the portico steps and went inside.

The foyer was empty, but voices resounded from the back of the house. Feeling adrift on uncertain seas with her eyes awash with tears, she paused at the foot of the main staircase and slipped out of her shoes. A snatch of conversation carried to her from the kitchen:

"If you're worried Jake's feelings toward you will change because he's met someone he cares for—"

"I'm not worried. And I'm not jealous, okay, Mom?" echoed Joy's caustic retort.

"You liked her at first. If you would give her a chance, I'm sure you could like her again."

"Like you and Dad?"

Oppressed by the weight of baggage before her time, Shelby crept up the stairs on soundless feet. Small children played on the second-floor landing. She stepped over their building blocks into the bathroom and sat down on the edge of the tub, elbows on her knees, hands cupping her chin. But the urge to cry had passed. Her ears had trapped Paula's words to Joy. Jake *did* care. She cared, too. So much, she had temporarily ceased to anguish over her creative blockage. Until Jake ran slipshod over the wound and the blood-letting began.

A gentle rap on the door brought Shelby's heart to her throat. "Who is it?"

"Jimmy. I got to go," a small voice replied from the other side of the door.

Shelby surrendered her hiding place to Jake's little nephew. She cast about for a quiet spot in which to sort conflicting feelings. Jake's door stood open. But it was the last place she cared to be found should he come looking. Likewise, the guest room, littered with luggage and Uncle Hershel's fiddle case was out of bounds. A third door revealed steep and narrow stairs.

Shelby flipped on the light and climbed to the attic. Sunshine poured from an open trapdoor in the attic ceiling. It lit her way past trunks and boxes and cast-off furnishings to a five-step fold-down ladder leading up the catwalk. She hesitated a moment, then climbed it to find a small patch of unadorned roof. There was no furniture, nothing on which to perch and nothing spectacular about the view—just tree-tops, the street and neighboring homes. Shelby was about to return the way she had come when a neon sign hanging from the wrought-iron railing caught her eye. Modest in size, it wasn't lighted. But on closer inspection, the message was perfectly legible. Jake's intentions, too. He wasn't joking with that implied, over-the-phone proposal. He *did* want to marry her. Tears stung her nose and filled her eyes. "Oh, Jake," she whispered, and ran her hands over the glass letters, in equal parts of joy and trepidation.

Chapter Nineteen

It was the quarrel in the yard, and the fuse that had ignited it that filled Shelby with misgivings. Had she not been so plain about keeping her unpublished work private, she could write Jake's trespass off as live and learn.

Maybe she should anyway. Jake hadn't known her then as he knew her now, Shelby tried to reason away doubt. They would talk. Lord willing, he would see that just as she would not presume to tell him how to do his job, she couldn't let him hamper hers by disregarding her established methods. So thinking, Shelby ignored the clamor of her first love, that jealous muse that shouted, *He'll destroy your writing. Just wait and see! The first time it gets in the way of what he wants, he'll expect you to give it up for him. He's just like Patrick.*

He isn't *anything* like Patrick, she thought wordlessly, and retraced her steps to the landing.

The tots had angled a storybook on the top step, and were using it as a ramp to slide their building blocks down the stairs. Concerned over the hazard the blocks presented to Gram and others using the stairs, Shelby resisted the urge to seek out Jake for bridge-mending.

"What a lovely book. Who wants to hear the story?" she said, and gently coerced the children into picking up their blocks.

Jake thanked the community one by one for coming to share the day with Gram Kate. Each hand he shook and each goodbye seemed like a stone on a rising wall that was blocking his way to Shelby. At long last, with only family remaining, he let himself into the kitchen where the women were transferring party leftovers from the refrigerator to the dinner table.

When Shelby turned with a dish of fresh fruit in her hands, Jake was there to take it. There was a searching light in the hazel eyes that darted to meet his gaze. Or was it discomfort over their quarrel? Uncertain, Jake murmured, "Still mad at me?"

"I don't want to be," she replied in quiet tones designed to keep it between them.

"I'm sorry."

But before he could say anything else, Paula brushed past, moving dishes and tableware.

"Have you seen Gram's glasses, Jake? She's misplaced them again."

Jake scoured the kitchen, the porch and the yard before Joy found the glasses in Gram's pocketbook. It was that kind of evening, and dark before he had a chance to be alone with Shelby.

"Sun's set. But it's a starry night, and worth seeing," he said, on the way upstairs.

"Where you going?" Joy called after them.

"Catwalk," Jake replied.

He smiled at Shelby. "Stairs are steep. Watch your step." He switched on the light and took her hand.

Midway to the attic, Shelby paused.

Jake stopped a step ahead and turned back. The naked overhead bulb cast him in garish light. *As did his deed.* Shelby couldn't just sweep it under so as to get on to the rooftop and horizons that beckoned with promises of having and holding and being held forever after with a man who would never let her cry in the dark alone. Struggling, she said, "Could we clear the air?"

"Now?" he asked.

"I'd like to." Shelby sought flame-retardant words so as to get to the heart of the matter without igniting sparks that could so easily burn their bridges. "I shouldn't have said what I did about Patrick this afternoon," she began.

"That I'm jealous?" said Jake. "I'm not."

"There's no reason for you to be," she said earnestly. "I was upset."

"I noticed. What is this love-hate thing you've got going?"

"I don't love him, Jake." Determined to have it said without being sidetracked from the real issue, Shelby admitted, "Not in the way that you mean. I can't hate him, either."

"I thought we'd finished with Patrick, I was talking about your writing."

"You were?" Relieved, she said, "That's good. Because that's what I want to talk about, too. When it comes to writing, I'm compelled. Books have always been my sanctuary."

"I was kind of hoping I could be that."

"My sanctuary?" she said in wonder.

"Your sanctuary." His voice was like a corn husk touched by early frost. His hands spanned her waist. The soft gleam in his eye pleaded be done with words.

Shelby rested her hands on his shoulders, a half measure between holding and being held. She teetered on the steps, relishing bone, sinew and muscle gathered beneath flesh-warmed cotton. Books weren't just her sanctuary, they had also become her solace. But Jake's fingers, tucking a curl behind her ear, caressing her cheek, obliterated the appeal of black type on crisp white pages.

She longed to tell him how storybooks had become both lap and latch string. But he had lost parents and seen his sister's marriage crumble in one fell swoop. His losses belittled her petty scrapes, for her parents were both well and well-intentioned and she had no siblings casting their cares on her. She said instead, "I respect the gift and I need you to respect it, too."

"I will. So long as it doesn't use you up until there's nothing left."

"For you?" she said, feeling her muse stir, hackles rising.

"Is that so selfish?" he countered. "I can tell you right now, if sign work ever gets to be the struggle for me that writing is for you, I'll give it up."

"It isn't in me to quit," she asserted, bidding his understanding. "Anyway, when a book is finished, it isn't the struggle I remember."

"Are you going to be able to finish this one?" Jake asked.

"I don't know," she admitted. "It was careless of me not to have safeguarded my work. But on your behalf, and Joy's, too, it was unfair of me to imply that your previewing in some way prevented me from moving ahead with the story."

"We'll do some more brainstorming, maybe we can jury-rig it," he said.

"It isn't as simple as a toggle switch gone awry," Shelby objected.

"So what do you suggest?" he asked.

"For starters, stay away from my works in progress and I'll stay out of your shop." She put it as simply and as nicely as she knew how.

"Not so fast," he objected and covered her hands to keep them from falling away from him. "You're welcome in my shop anytime."

"Jake, don't make this more difficult than it has to be. You know what I'm saying."

"Sanctified. Set apart. No Jake allowed?"

"It safeguards the process," she reasoned. "Then, if I hit a brick wall, I know it isn't because I ignored what works. That's not unreasonable, is it?"

"No, not in theory," he replied. "Come on up on the roof. I want to show you something."

"As soon as we settle this."

"I thought we just did," he said.

"Then you understand that I need some privacy while I'm working?"

"For how long?" he asked.

"However long it takes to grow words into something ready for publication."

"At which point you share it with how many million readers?" he asked.

"Tens of millions would be a dream come true," she said.

Jake saw her color deepen, and knew he'd caught her fantasizing. It frustrated him that she could bare her soul to readers and be so reluctant to let him in. He was thinking how to ask why that was so when Joy called to him from the landing. She had the portable phone in one hand and covered the receiver with the other.

"It's for you, Uncle Jake. I think it's important. Whoever it is, she's asking about Dad."

Defeated, Jake sighed. "Do you mind, Shelby?"

"No, go ahead."

Jake glanced back to see Shelby sit down on the steps and hug her knees. Something in her eyes and the downward sweep of her lashes brought a knot to his throat. If not for Joy and the call to which he was now obligated, he would forego ambiance, starlight and neon and propose on the spot before the Jackson clan started looking like a pill she couldn't swallow. "As soon as I'm done here, we'll finish this uninterrupted, okay?"

"Okay," she agreed, with a tentative smile that squeezed his heart even as he turned away to take the call.

"Jake Jackson speaking. I'm sorry, I can't hear you. Hold on, and I'll try an extension."

"Battery must be low." Jake started down the stairs, glanced back and held up a finger to indicate he'd return in a moment.

Hedged in by the proposal waiting above, Shelby's misgivings gave doubts a leg up and over the hastily constructed white picket fence about her heart. She loved him. And he loved her. Yet he had said in essence that he would quit rather than struggle through when the joy went out of his work. Would his attitude hinder his tolerance toward her writing when she hit stubborn patches? Did that explain this crowdedness? This press of doubt? Jake's work was straightforward and logical. He would not forever acquiesce to the demands of her muse, demands which defied logic and challenged explanation.

"So, what'd you tell him?" Joy broke the silence.

Shelby started. Sifting her thoughts, she had forgotten Joy there at the foot of the attic steps. "Tell him?" she echoed. "About what?"

A shrewd expression stole over Joy's face. "Never mind. I smell popcorn. You coming down?"

Shrinking from doubts exposed beneath the dim light of the staircase, Shelby came to her feet and followed Joy downstairs. The front door stood open. A clear invitation. Her hat was there on the deacon's bench just inside the door.

"Where you going?" asked Joy.

"It's been a long day. When Jake gets off the phone, tell him I've gone, would you please?"

"Okay, sure. Mom'll be along soon as she gets Gram to bed. There's a key under the mat, if the door's locked," Joy said.

Shelby didn't correct her assumption that she meant to stay the night at Joy's home. Until she could lay her fears to rest and say in all confidence that she could and would and very much wanted to be Jake's wife, she was less than Jake needed her to be. It wasn't fair to let him show his heart only to be put on hold while she made up her mind which she wanted most: her writing, or Jake. In essence, that's what he was asking—the right to be the only one left standing. *If it came to that.* And who knew better than she just how easily it could?

Jake took the call in his study.

"Mr. Jackson? This is Monique Lockwood. We met at the mission last weekend. Mr. Weaver gave me your number. He said you had asked about Jig-Saw. You *do* know Jig-Saw?"

"Yes, I know him. But I'm not sure I can help you."

"I can understand how you might be reluctant to pass along information to a stranger," Monique said at his guardedness. "But I'd appreciate it if you would hear me out."

"Very well," Jake replied.

"Jig-Saw would like to see his daughter, now that he's more fully recovered."

"Recovered?" Jake echoed, sifting her voice for clues.

"From his accident. I assumed you knew about that."

"Very little," Jake admitted.

"The bottom line is, he's jobless and penniless and trying hard to get back on his feet. In the meantime, he would like to use my apartment as home base. Just for a day, long enough to have a nice visit with his daughter."

She paused. Jake volunteered nothing.

"In your opinion, would I be safe in letting him stay?" she continued.

"You're asking me if he's dangerous?" Jake queried.

"Exactly."

"If you don't know him any better than that, why

would you consider opening your home to him?''
Jake wondered, mystified.

"I've been in desperate need myself, and received
help with no motives beyond simple kindness. You
understand?''

"I'm trying to," Jake said. Picking words care-
fully, he offered, "The guy I knew wouldn't be a
risk to your property or your safety. But it was years
ago that I thought I knew him.''

"May I ask what your relationship to him was in
the past?''

Jake turned as Joy let herself into his office. "I'm
not free to say.''

"All right. I think I understand. Thank you for
your time.''

Joy glanced at the Caller ID as Jake was hanging
up the phone. "Who is she?" she asked.

"Someone wanting to know about your dad,"
Jake replied.

"I *know* that much. Did you tell her that him and
Mom are still married?'' Joy asked.

Hope was a stubborn thing in the heart of a child.
It seemed cruel to uproot it. Jake said, "All she
wanted was a character reference.''

"So that's it." Joy reached for a stickie note and
a pen. "Shelby went home.''

"Home?" Distracted from pursuing her note taking, Jake asked, "What for?''

"Long day is all she said. I told her where we
hide the door key.''

Jake was almost to the corridor when Joy asked,
"What'd she think of your sign?''

Pained, he turned back. "Let me guess—you
showed her?''

"Not on your life. She took herself up."

"You saw her go?"

"No. But Jimmy and the others did. Earlier. They were playing on the landing."

"You're sure about this?"

Joy nodded. "Kind of nervy of her, huh? Poking around after making such a big deal over us reading her story."

"How long ago did she leave?" Jake asked.

"Five minutes, thereabouts."

Jake crossed to the desk and dialed Paula's house. It rang unanswered. "What else did she say?" Jake queried, hanging up as Paula's answering machine clicked on.

"Nothing. Where're you going?"

"Your house."

"What for?"

"I'm going to marry that woman, that's what for."

Jake left Joy so that he could take down the number from caller ID and drove over to Paula's. Shelby's car wasn't there.

Jake circled the village until his sinking heart could no longer avoid the truth. Shelby had left Liberty Flats. Working through to the inevitable conclusion, he thought about taking the interstate north and going after her. But why drive like a madman just to hear what her absence said so clearly?

Jake returned home but couldn't bring himself to go inside. He sat on the porch a foot from where Uncle Hershel had plied him with advice. If it wasn't so gut-wrenching, it would be poetic. Not the part he had heard. Rather, the part about taking Shelby into consideration. Even Joy had assumed he would. A week ago, when she had asked if he would be moving to Chicago, he had chuckled. His roots were here. He had obligations he couldn't and had no wish to abandon.

It was that which kept Jake on the porch in stubborn resistance to his heart's entreaty until the deep night dampness finally drove him inside. Concern couldn't be shut off like a tap just because hope had dwindled to one thin drip. It was a long drive home, and she was tired. Jake phoned and left a message asking her to call him when she arrived so he wouldn't worry. From there, it was a waiting game. He propped his feet on his desk and leaned back in his chair.

It was daylight when Jake awoke to the ringing phone. Heart slamming, he was wide awake in an instant. But it was Paula calling to remind Joy that the youth group were serving pancakes before Sunday school.

"I'll tell her," Jake promised.

The sofa was empty. Joy had left a note, saying she had left for the youth group pancake breakfast fund-raiser. Gram, Uncle Hershel and Aunt Marge were dressed for church, drinking coffee as they waited for the appointed pancake hour.

Jake climbed the stairs and showered and shaved. The mirror was a steamy prism multiplying endless years of showering and shaving to meet a day like the last one. Because the woman who prided herself on not being a quitter had stolen his future on the way out the door.

But there was a door in. Jake took it on his knees, and rose with a clearer idea of stones left unturned. Yes, he and Shelby were worlds apart in some ways. Yes, there would always be conflicts. But he wasn't

Colt, and she wasn't Paula. They weren't quitters. They shared a center. That center was more than love, it was God Himself.

Hope restored, Jake retrieved his sign from the roof and put it in the back of the Jeep. A few miles past Bloomington, he reached for his cell phone only to realize he had left it in one of the work trucks. Uncle Hershel and Aunt Marge would be leaving after lunch, and someone needed to be at the house with Gram. Unwilling to turn back for the phone, Jake reasoned he could call home from Shelby's. His family would all be in church by now, anyway.

Chapter Twenty

Shelby crawled out of bed and into the shower. Steamy water and scented gel soap did little to ease her inner pain. *If sign work ever gets to be the struggle for me that writing is for you, I'll give it up.* Jake's words played in her head like a runner jogging in place, trampling dreams underfoot.

How could she give up writing? It was like asking a bird not to fly. Shelby shut off the water tap, toweled off and slipped into a soft pink robe. She then checked her phone messages. Jake's voice on her machine broke the silence of her apartment and brought a wave of pain that was both emotional and physical. She played the message a second time.

"It's a long drive to make twice in one day. Call and let me know you're home safely."

He would want to know why she had left without a word. What was she supposed to tell him? The truth, scolded her muse. Tell him the truth! There isn't room for him.

She reached for the phone, and had second

thoughts. Maybe a fax? No, that was worse than ignoring the message altogether. Her pulse pounded as she dialed. Jake's machine picked up. She hung up without leaving a message, thought a moment how to word what needed saying, and redialed only to lose courage again.

"This is all your fault," Shelby muttered to the short shelf of teen novels displayed on the wall over the living room nook where she did her writing. "You're supposed to inspire me, not sabotage my life. Look at me! I'm talking to books."

Pitiful!

Before she could follow through with her intent to call, someone knocked at her door. Heart in her throat, she rose on tiptoes, looked through the peephole and gaped with wondering eyes. "Joy!" She gasped and slid the dead bolt free.

"I'm alone," said Joy, wise to Shelby's darting glance down the empty corridor.

"How did you get here?" blurted Shelby.

"Uncle Jake had a service job."

"On Sunday?"

"It was an emergency. You said drop by if I got to Chicago. So here I am," she said with a vagrant grin.

Reeling with misgivings, Shelby framed and discarded half a dozen questions in the time it took Joy to step inside and drop her overnight bag in the entry foyer. "Call your mother, and let her know you arrived safely," she said, and closed the door.

Joy tugged at her rumpled sweatshirt and tilted one shoulder. "She's probably already left for church."

"Try her anyway," Shelby said. "Have you eaten?"

"Not yet."

"I'll fix you some breakfast while you're on the phone."

"Okay. Can I use your bathroom?" Joy asked.

"Yes, of course. Through the living room and to your left."

"I like my eggs hard." Joy picked up the portable phone on her way by.

Cheeky little thing, of course she did.

Shelby waited until the bathroom door closed, then returned to the foyer to look inside the canvas bag. She found a round-trip bus ticket from Bloomington to Chicago, with the return ticket still to be redeemed. How had Joy had traveled the twenty miles between Liberty Flats and Bloomington? Anyone's guess. Hearing Joy on the phone, Shelby replaced the ticket, trekked into the kitchen and quietly picked up the extension.

"Okay, Mom. Yeah, Uncle Jake dropped me off." Joy carried on a one-sided conversation. "She's fixing breakfast for me now. But I'll tell her you said hello. Love you, too. Bye."

Shelby had eggs, toast, cereal and juice waiting by the time Joy joined her in the kitchen.

"Mom says hi. What happened to you last night?" Joy shoveled in eggs and chewed and sipped her juice, looking vaguely discomfited. "It wasn't anything I said made you go, was it?" she asked finally.

"My coming home had nothing to do with you."

"That's good. 'Cause last night, Uncle Jake was all set to blame me."

"And this morning?"

"I don't know, I left before he got—" Joy

blinked. Had she slapped her hand over her gaping mouth, it couldn't have been more telling.

"That's what I thought," Shelby said, a dull pounding at her temples. "You want to tell me what you're really doing here?"

Joy's chin came up. Her shoulders, too. "Okay, so I came to see my dad."

"He's expecting you?" Shelby asked, struggling to remain calm.

"No. Not yet. But a friend of his knows I'm here. She's trying to get in touch with him and let him know I'm here. I wouldn't have bothered you, but I don't know anyone else in Chicago."

Shelby remembered Jig-Saw's request of Monique at Can-Do and thanked God that Joy had trusted her enough to seek her out rather than kill time on her own on the streets of Chicago. "This friend—she's going to call you here?"

Joy nodded.

Shelby sipped her coffee and traced the cup rim with her finger. "Let me see if I have this right— you're letting go of your mother and Jake and Gram Kate and the rest of your family to make room for your father?" she queried, trying her hand at psychology.

"Well, no. I'm taking the bus back tomorrow."

"What if they don't want you back? What if they say, you made your choice, live with it?"

Joy looked at her as if she had the brain power of a staple. "Yeah, right. Like they're really going to do that."

"Call and let them know you're safe."

"I called."

"No, you didn't. I listened. That was a dial tone you were talking to."

Joy's eyes glittered. "You're a sneak."

"That's right. We're both sneaks. Now, do you want to call home, or shall I do it for you?"

"Oh, all right. So it was a bad idea. Forget the whole thing. Dad can come see me in Liberty Flats. Mom will just *love* that," she said, rolling her eyes.

Shelby ignored her theatrics and crossed to the wall phone. "What's your home number? I'll punch it in for you," she said, and passed Joy the receiver.

Paula's shout of mingled relief and distress was loud enough to be heard without the phone. "Joy? Thank God! Where are you? I've been worried sick."

Joy set her jaw, insisting that she wanted to see her dad. Whatever Paula's response, Joy received it with undisguised impatience "Okay, Mom. I heard you the first time," she said and passed the phone to Shelby. "She wants to talk to you."

"Shelby? I'm coming for her," Paula said, her voice high and tight.

"I can put her on a bus, train or plane, and save you the trip," Shelby offered.

"No, no. I'll come," Paula cried. "I'm sorry to put you in the middle of this. But just don't let her leave, okay?"

Shelby promised. She poured herself a second cup of coffee and had no more than sat down, when the phone rang again.

"I'll get it." Joy nearly knocked over her chair, in her rush to answer it. "Yeah, it's me, Joy. Can I talk to him? Oh." Joy's face fell. "Well, okay. Thanks, anyway."

"Let me talk," Shelby offered, reaching for the receiver.

"Too late," Joy said, hanging up the phone. "That was Dad's friend. Dad can't make it today."

Shelby saw her slump in disappointment, and still, she wasn't entirely sure Joy was telling her the truth. Reluctant to leave her unattended for the short time it would take to throw on some clothes, Shelby winged silent petitions to God as she washed and dried the dishes. Joy watched the clock.

"You're welcome to turn on the television," Shelby said.

"No, thanks."

"How about a book?"

"I'm fine."

Shelby offered another diversionary idea or two, then gave up. Joy drummed her fingers on the table-top. With the morning stretching endlessly before her, Shelby resorted to the panacea for whatever ailed and sat down at her laptop.

On impulse, she tried Jake's idea about writing the ending. That, at least, was firmly set in her mind. Fingers poised over the keys, she opened the tap and let her thoughts flow.

The rest of Tara and Jack's day passed in a blur. Their statement at the police station. The piecing together of details. And finally, after dinner, a little time to themselves. They left Jack's house behind and walked toward the music and the lights on the square downtown where Blatchford's street festival was in full swing.

"You want to ride some rides?" Jack asked, as they neared the Ferris wheel with its flashing lights.

"Sure," said Tara.

"Come on, and we'll get some tickets."

Jack caught Tara's hand in his and whistled off-key as they strolled along.

"Jack and Tara? That's how this turns out? Bummer!" Joy complained, reading over Shelby's shoulder. "I thought he liked Cheryl."

"He did. But it didn't work," Shelby said.

"Why not?"

"Because they aren't right for one another. So he had a change of heart."

Feeling hopeful now that words were finally flowing, Shelby relegated Joy's voice to background noise and scrolled back to the scene where Tara and Jack discovered Mr. Weedman's body.

She worked doggedly, adding then deleting words and dialogue and paragraphs until the whole screen was a mess. She sat back in the chair, defeated once again.

"Looks to me like you're stuck in the field with a dead body and getting nowhere fast," Joy crowed.

"That's about the size of it." Shelby sighed. "The kids should be shocked and scared and feel the loss."

"Like when I heard about Mr. Wiseman," Joy said, nodding.

Shelby turned back to the screen. "I can get the shocked and scared part, it's the loss that eludes me. I was hoping it would go easier, now that I have the ending down. But I still can't get it right."

"Want me to give it a go?" Joy offered.

Shelby didn't expect her to be of much help. But at this point, she was amenable to anything that would shed light on what was missing. "Be my guest," she said, and gave up the chair.

Joy's hands fell over the keyboard and hovered a moment. At length she typed: "It was like the day I found out my dad didn't know about me. I was dead to him. But this guy was *dead* dead. I cried."

The switch to first person jarred Shelby. The voice was not hers. But the emotion was so real, her story world fell away, leaving only Joy, cherished by her mother, awash with family, and still needy. It was almost as if she had stepped into Joy's head and was seeing her neediness from the inside.

A neediness Jake wasn't meant to fill. Jig-Saw himself couldn't, though as the missing piece, he distracted Joy from letting God's love fill the void. *But who was she to tell Joy?* Shelby read it over again, this time with the heat of repentance behind her eyes.

Somewhere in the neighborhood, church bells rang. Shelby moved to the window of her corner apartment and found a steeple on the horizon. "He does not dwell in temples built by hands." Snatches of remembered verse fell to mind. "In him we live and move and have our being."

How could she have relegated her first love to second place? It wasn't books, it was God! He was the lap in the story when she was a child. He was the flame when her muse burned the brightest. It was so blessedly simple. How could she have been so mistaken? And at what price?

"What's the matter?"

Shelby glanced around to find Joy watching from the desk chair. "It's good, what you wrote."

"Really?" Joy couldn't hide her pleasure. "Must have got it from Dad."

Shelby remembered Jake telling her Colton had been a young journalist in pursuit of a story when he first met Paula. Shelby wiped her eyes before turning to face Joy. "Maybe you should finish it."

"Huh?"

"The story," Shelby said, the idea gaining strength. "Would you like to finish it?"

"How? You wrote it. It's yours."

"It doesn't have to be. I could give it to you."

Joy shift uneasily. "Just like that?"

"You inspired it. I've beat myself up trying to finish it to no avail." *And in the process neglected a greater love.* Fresh tears stung Shelby's eyes. "Play with it, see what you think."

Joy turned back to the computer screen.

Oh, God. Forgive me! I'm just a little child. But I'm Your *little child. Tell me it isn't too late!* The joyous peal of bells swelled as if carrying her prayer along.

The paperboy was whistling his way down the corridor just beyond the front door. Shelby heard him trade greetings with someone as the newspaper thudded against the door.

With Joy engrossed at the computer, Shelby retrieved the paper from the hallway. She was about to close the door when an out-of-place red glare at the end of the hall caught her eye. There was a table of potted plants next to the elevator. Above it hung a neon question: Marry Me? Jake was hunkered down, his back to her, picking up sign-hanging tools.

Dust motes danced over his head in a shaft of sunlight from the eastern window. A mountain moved off Shelby's heart and slipped past the tears in her throat. She was about to duck inside and trade her robe for something more suitable when Jake came to his feet and stepped into the open elevator.

"Jake! Wait!" she cried, dismayed to see him leaving.

Jake scanned the panel for the door control button. Shelby was taking no chances. She plowed through the closing gap into the elevator. "Where are you going?"

"Down," he said.

"Without a word?" Shelby cried, arms crossed, hugging her waist.

"I was coming right—" he began. Then he caught himself, and said, "I've had my word. It was lit up in red, in case you missed it."

"I didn't miss it. You didn't give me a chance to answer."

"Me? What about you? You took off last night before I could ask."

"You're right. I'm sorry. I was so confused." Trembling, she leaned against the wall as the elevator took them down.

"Joy said you'd seen the sign. So when you left, I figured that was your answer." Jake nudged his cap back and shifted his feet. "I had a little talk with myself, and decided maybe that as package deals go, we Jacksons are high maintenance. But there's no reason I couldn't move part of the sign business here to Chicago. We could keep your apartment, take our turn with Gram in Liberty Flats and stay here the rest of the time. I haven't talked to my sisters about it yet, but they've always done their part." The elevator stopped. The door opened. Their fingers brushed as they reached at the same moment to hit the "3" button.

"You thought I left because I didn't want to share your family?" she said, slowly taking it in, as the elevator reversed its course.

"That wasn't it?"

"No, of course not! Jake, I had no idea you thought that."

"What is it, then? You just don't want to marry me?"

"That isn't it at all." Shelby's eye drew tears. She fought them back. "I thought I had to make a choice."

She was captivating, wrapped in a deep flush and a fuzzy robe. It was a sight he could drink in for a lifetime of mornings. And nights, too. He tensed, waiting for the picture to cloud. But she didn't mention Gram Kate, Joy, Paula or any of his clamoring clan. Instead, she spoke of worrying that anything that got in the way of her writing would get in the way of her wholeness.

"And you thought *I* was in the way?" He finally caught her drift.

"Yes," she admitted. "But I had it backward. My writing was getting in the way of living. I don't want to lose you, Jake. You're so precious to me," she said earnestly.

A wave of tenderness swept over him at the glimpse of her exposed heart. He cupped her ears and tipped her face. "Is that a yes?"

Even her toes were tinted pink. They wiggled fetchingly as she closed the remaining step and leaned in to kiss a smile to his face.

The elevator whispered to a stop, cutting short their reconciliation. Jake nudged her ahead with a hand on the small of her back. She paused to pull the Yes chain on the neon sign, then turned with a seeking light in her hazel eyes.

"Now you're talking." Jake swept her off her feet and carried her down the hallway.

"Practice run," he said, and laughed when she protested.

But once inside the door, Jake saw she had company and set her down in a hurry. "Joy!"

"Hi, Uncle Jake. Mom send you?"

"What're you doing here?"

"Writing," Joy said. She threw a glance over her shoulder. "Say, I've been meaning to ask—is nightshade fatal to people, too?"

Shelby excused herself, ducked into her bedroom to dress, and left them to sort it out. When she returned, Joy had dragged herself away from the computer and was chewing her nails down to the quick. Jake was on the phone with Paula en route to Chicago. He told her she could turn back, that Joy could return home with him.

Shelby decided a little makeup would do no harm. She ducked into her bedroom and didn't come out until she heard the door slam.

Jake nudged his cap back as she slipped out again. He leaned against the closed door, ankles crossed, watching her approach. Her heart turned at the tender devotion on his face.

"Joy's checking out the sign," he said, and reached for her hand.

"She hasn't given up the idea of seeing her father, Jake," Shelby warned, clutching his fingers.

"Relax, she's on good behavior. Paula's reconsidered," he said, and sandwiched her hand between his.

"She's going to let Joy visit Colton?" asked Shelby.

"Paula wants to size him up first. If he doesn't run afoul of her maternal instincts, it could be a new beginning. For Joy and Colt, anyway," Jake amended. He kissed her, and traced with his fingertip the lips he had warmed. "Speaking of new beginnings, I've been thinking about your story world."

"What about it?" she asked.

"I'll leave it to you, and be the happiest guy around, just as long as there is always room for me in your real world."

"It would be empty space without you, Billy Boy."

A light leapt behind his bottle-blue eyes. "Keep that up, and you'll have to learn to use that rolling pin," he warned.

"For what?" she asked with an innocent tilt of her face.

Jake spelled it out in kisses that deepened until the world fell away leaving only the two of them. Shelby's heart sang in anticipation of that celebrated day when their lives would be truly one. It raised such a clamor, she didn't hear Joy return until she cleared her throat noisily.

"Don't mind me," Joy said, rolling her eyes.

"We're trying not to," Jake said. He pressed a kiss to the palm of Shelby's hand before letting her go.

Shelby stored away the sensation in the treasure trove where the richest of ideas germinated. As she did so, the love God had given her for Jake dispelled every concern over her future as a writer. Whatever she gave, he gave back to her, multiplied in emotions so lavish in detail, it would take her a lifetime to get it all down.

"I love you, Jake. I'll be in the kitchen," she whispered, and slipped off to hide the rolling pin.

Epilogue

Shelby awoke ahead of her alarm. She slipped out of bed and threw the drapes wide. A marry-me sunrise pinked the sky and polished the lake. Kneeling, she thanked God for this, her wedding day. For the story proposal that had been accepted by her publisher. For May flowers blooming on the shores of Lake Michigan where she and Jake were to be wed. And most of all, for Jake.

She soaked in a scented bath, then dressed in a jade-colored sheath and stole a moment to thumb through her pile of greeting cards.

There was one from Monique, who had moved out of state last fall, and another from Patrick who wrote that he was leaving his law practice to attend seminary. There was a card from Joy as well, one she had made on her computer. In it, she wrote that her father was going to help her with the Weed Buster book, but that they hadn't made much progress yet, as they were doing their cowriting by e-mail. Same old Joy, Shelby thought with a faint smile. Paula gave an inch, granting Colton biweekly visitation rights, and Joy wanted a mile, begging her to let her father come for the summer, now that he was well again and gainfully employed.

The doorbell stirred Shelby from her musings. It was her parents with the pastor in tow. Her mother helped Shelby arrange her hair in a tumble of loose curls and a simple garland of May flowers.

"It looks as if she's going through with it this time," her father remarked to the minister when Shelby emerged from the bedroom.

"At long last, your chance to give me away," she said, and pinned a carnation to his lapel.

"Look at her glow!" her mother said to her father.

"I'd glow, too, if I could quit my job and move to the country," replied her father.

"I haven't quit writing. And Liberty Flats isn't country living, it's a village," Shelby said. Her notice, given at Parnell Publishing two weeks earlier, had been met with kind wishes for her future as a full-time wife and a part-time novelist.

The phone rang. Her mother answered it. "Hello, Jake. Yes, she's right here."

Shelby took the portable phone.

"Hi, honey," Jake's voice stroked her ear. "Look out your east window."

Shelby took the phone to her bedroom, glimpsed a man looking back at her through her third-story window and let out a yelp.

"Ouch!" Jake, just outside her window, held the phone away and wiggled his finger in his ear.

"You scared the wits out of me!" Recovering, Shelby put the phone down to open the window. Jake was standing on the platform at the top of the ladder extending from one of the company trucks parked in the lot below. "Is that our honeymoon transportation?" she asked.

"The Jeep had a flat," he teased, and leaned through the open window for a kiss.

"Please please climb in here," pleaded Shelby, gripping the lapels of his tuxedo. "You'll give me a heart attack on my wedding day."

"Speaking of hearts, I seem to recall yours was secretly set on elopement," Jake said, coming through the window. "A ladder is a nice concession."

"You surely don't plan to take me down that ladder!" she cried.

"What? You don't trust me?"

Relishing the love in those summer-sky eyes, Shelby came to terms accordingly. She let the repressed actress out of the box, saying, "Very well, then. But if we're going to put on a show, I'll have to change into satin and lace."

He crooked an eyebrow. "You don't mean the wedding dress?"

"Isn't that why I kept it—for a better man?"

Jake laughed and kissed her and let her go. She rubbed away the painted lips she had left on his mouth, and pointed him toward the living room to usher her father and Pastor Fuller downstairs while her mother helped her change into the wedding dress.

Twenty minutes later, Shelby was tucked firmly in Jake's arms on the small platform at the top of the ladder. She clutched his arm, her long white skirts and her bouquet of sunflowers. With a radiant smile, she tilted her face to the lakeshore breeze. It rearranged her curls and set her skirts to rustling.

"You're drawing a crowd in that dress," Jake said.

Shelby stole a kiss for courage and looked down. Her eyes welled up at the sight of their loved ones intermingled below, smiling and waving, celebrating this long-awaited day.

On cue from below, Jake manned the controls. "Love me?" he asked in a tender voice.

"Forever," she promised and kissed him all the way to the ground.

*   *   *   *   *

Dear Reader,

When I was a little girl practicing piano and missing more notes than I hit, my father would call out, "Would you play 'Long, Long Ago and Far, Far Away'?" At the time, his humor was lost on me. Now as a writer I smile over the irony that I should so often inhabit Storyland, that set-apart place that is often "Long, Long Ago" and always "Far, Far Away."

It opened to me first in daydreams and childhood games of "dress up" and "pretend." Now, as a writer, I find that the God-given link between daydreaming and plotting a story is very clear to me. Thanks to Him and to readers, I have license to daydream! Which makes Shelby's world familiar territory. Like her, I spend my days shifting from reality to fiction and back again. It's a dance, and I'm not all that graceful. But I *am* grateful to family and friends who overlook my absenteeism and wait for me to catch the next thought-wave home. For as much as I enjoy creating story worlds, home is my most cherished place this side of heaven, as I'm sure is true for you, too.

Susan Kirby

Take 2 inspirational love stories FREE!

PLUS get a FREE surprise gift!

Special Limited-Time Offer

Mail to Steeple Hill Reader Service™

In U.S.	In Canada
3010 Walden Ave.	P.O. Box 609
P.O. Box 1867	Fort Erie, Ontario
Buffalo, NY 14240-1867	L2A 5X3

YES! Please send me 2 free Love Inspired® novels and my free surprise gift. Then send me 3 brand-new novels every month, which I will receive months before they appear in bookstores. Bill me at the low price of $3.74 each in the U.S. and $3.96 each in Canada, plus 25¢ delivery and applicable sales tax, if any*. That's the complete price and a saving of over 10% off the cover prices—quite a bargain! I understand that accepting the books and gift places me under no obligation ever to buy any books. I can always return a shipment and cancel at any time. Even if I never buy another book from Steeple Hill, the 2 free books and the surprise gift are mine to keep forever.

303 IEN CM6R
103 IEN CM6Q

Name	(PLEASE PRINT)	
Address	Apt. No.	
City	State/Prov.	Zip/Postal Code

* Terms and prices are subject to change without notice. Sales tax applicable in New York. Canadian residents will be charged applicable provincial taxes and GST. All orders subject to approval. Offer limited to one per household.

INTLI-299   ©1998